"Oh, Lord," Dana whispered

Suddenly her insides were hurting.

"That's right. I'd give anything not to have to shock you like this, but…"

She wrapped her arms around her chest, still reeling from her father's news.

"You see—"

She did her utmost to concentrate as he began speaking once more, but she could barely make out what he was saying because her ears were ringing.

It was something about the name Haine.

Listen, she ordered herself. *Pay attention. Keep your emotions in check.*

That last one was impossible, but she tried as hard as she could.

"That's when I had to tell you," her father was continuing. "Because the other day, the very first time I saw you and Noah together…the way you look at each other…"

"Is it that obvious?" she murmured.

"Uh-huh."

But of course it was. Noah was the love of her life. Now, though…

Dear Reader,

One of the things I tell my students in the romance writing course I teach is not to make things easy for their characters. When it came to Dana Morancy, I took that advice seriously.

We all have emotional baggage, but I gave her some that most of us would never dream of. Then I introduced her to the man she'd been waiting for her entire adult life—but put such a sharp twist in the road that just when she thinks she's looking straight at the "happy-ever-after," she discovers that things haven't been at all what they seemed.

As for Noah Haine, when the story begins the last thing he wants in his life is a woman. By the time it ends, it's the only thing he wants. And the woman has to be Dana—despite the complications.

I hope you enjoy the twists and turns of Dana and Noah's story.

Warmest wishes,

Dawn Stewardson

P.S. Please come and visit me at www.superauthors.com

Unexpected Outcome
Dawn Stewardson

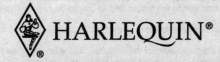

HARLEQUIN®

TORONTO • NEW YORK • LONDON
AMSTERDAM • PARIS • SYDNEY • HAMBURG
STOCKHOLM • ATHENS • TOKYO • MILAN • MADRID
PRAGUE • WARSAW • BUDAPEST • AUCKLAND

ISBN 0-373-71048-8

UNEXPECTED OUTCOME

Visit us at www.eHarlequin.com

Printed in U.S.A.

To John, always.

And to my editor, Beverley Sotolov,
who pushed me to write this particular book.

CHAPTER ONE

DANA WAITED WHILE Robert Haine settled himself in a visitors' chair, absently wondering why he'd come to see her.

Usually, a prospective client told her a bit about his problem when he called to make an appointment, but Haine hadn't given her the slightest clue.

He finally looked across the desk and said, "You were highly recommended, Ms. Morancy."

She smiled. "That's good to hear. Who should I thank?"

"I'm afraid I can't say. I didn't do the asking around myself. But I understand it was someone on the NYPD. An officer you used to work with."

While she nodded acknowledgement of that, she did her best to ignore the familiar chill creeping through her.

An officer she'd worked with. Someone who knew she hadn't been able to cut it on the job.

She stopped herself right there. Whoever had recommended her obviously thought she was a good private investigator. Despite her failings as a cop.

Forcing her full attention back to the moment, she said, "And what can I help you with, Mr. Haine?"

"Why don't we drop the formality. Go with Robert and Dana."

"Fine."

As he took a few seconds to choose his next words, she eyed him surreptitiously. In his midfifties, he was roughly the same age as her father—but she suspected that might be the only thing the two had in common.

They were certainly on different pages when it came to clothes. Her dad always claimed he felt uncomfortable in a suit. Robert Haine, wearing a perfectly cut charcoal pinstripe, clearly didn't.

"My business partner, Larry Benzer, and I have a company," he said at last. "Four Corners Imports. Someone is trying to sabotage it."

"I see," she said slowly. "Sabotage it how?"

"Various ways. Arson in our warehouse. A couple of cargo containers that simply vanished—which left us scrambling to supply our clients. Invoices that were printed but somehow didn't make it into the mail.

"Other things, too. Enough to affect both our bottom line and our reputation."

"And you're sure you haven't just had a string of bad luck?"

He shook his head. "Our employees seem to figure that's all it is. But only Larry and I are aware of *everything* that's been going on. And seeing the complete picture, we're convinced someone's out to get us.

"So is my nephew, Noah Haine, who's our director of finance."

"I see," she said again.

"The three of us have been spending half our time trying to figure out who it is. But the only thing we're agreed on is that it has to be someone with access to inside information."

"Someone on your staff, then."

"That's the obvious conclusion," he said, his expression telling her how much that bothered him.

"Are you particularly suspicious of anyone?"

"There are a few people it *could* be. Theoretically speaking. But when it comes to hard evidence…"

He shrugged, indicating they had none, so she said, "What about a possible motive?"

"Again, only a couple of theories."

"Theories are a good place to start. Why don't you tell me what they are."

After a moment's hesitation, he said, "Well, you'll need a little background information to understand the first one.

"A few years ago, Larry and I decided to expand into the West Coast market. That took money, so we went public to raise it.

"The shares did fine right from the initial offering, but in the past while they've dropped through the floor. Because, as I said, these problems have cost us money.

"But the point is, we figure someone could be accumulating shares on the cheap. And when he's got enough the sabotage will miraculously stop. Then he'll sell after the price recovers."

Dana nodded, thinking nobody orchestrating a scheme like that would be dumb enough to purchase shares in his own name. Or *her* own, as the case might be. But there could easily be an accomplice with no apparent link to the company.

"Our other idea," Robert was saying, "is that a competitor's trying to drive us out of business. And has a Four Corners employee on its payroll."

"Do you have many competitors?"

"Only two major ones. We're a niche company— import collectibles and sell them almost exclusively to interior design firms."

After another brief silence, he added, "Is this the sort of job you'd take on?"

"Yes. Definitely." White-collar crime. No risk of shoot-'em-ups. Tailor-made for Dana Morancy.

"I'd just like to ask a few more questions," she continued. "Exactly who knows you're hiring a private investigator?"

"Right now, nobody except Larry and me. We'll tell my nephew, of course, but he's out of town until tomorrow."

She thought for a moment, then said, "How would you feel about *not* telling him? About not telling *anyone* else who I really am?"

Robert didn't seem to like the suggestion, so she said, "If one of your employees *is* involved, introducing me as a P.I. would warn him off. And if he goes to ground I'll have a harder time learning who he is."

"Yes, of course," he said slowly. "That makes sense. But what does it have to do with not telling Noah?"

"When you're trying to keep a secret, the fewer people in on it the better. All it takes is one slip…"

"Hmm…I see what you mean."

She waited, letting him debate with himself. She never pushed clients very hard on issues like this. That way, the decisions didn't come back to bite her.

"Okay," he said at last. "Only Larry and I will know. But if we don't say you're a P.I., how *do* we explain you?"

"Well, I've established an identity for undercover work—Dana Mayfield, an organizational design consultant. It's solidly backed up, so it checks out as authentic if anyone gets curious."

"A consultant," he repeated.

"Uh-huh. You've had this run of trouble, so you bring in a consultant. Your people would see that as a reasonable move, wouldn't they?"

"I guess *most* of them would. Noah, though…one of the first things he'll ask is whether we told you we think the problems are more than simple bad luck, that we're convinced someone's behind them. He'll figure that otherwise we're just wasting money."

"But logically, you *would* have told me. I mean, you'd have at least raised it as a possibility, wouldn't you?"

"Yes, you're right. So…how would this be? We say that we mentioned it, but didn't tell you we're pretty well certain—because we want you starting out with an open mind."

"Good. That sounds believable."

Robert nodded, then said, "Okay, that's how we'll handle it. And so that I don't come off looking like an idiot, I guess the next thing we need to talk about is what an organizational design consultant does. I only have a vague idea."

She gave him a smile. "You and just about everyone else. Which makes it a great cover. I can ask practically anything without raising suspicions.

"But, basically, a real OD person would look at the various structures in your company—reporting relationships, processes and systems, then recommend ways to improve them.

"So I'd be talking to your employees about their jobs. And the business in general. Asking for their input on how to make things work better."

"And while you're doing that you're hoping someone says something…incriminating?"

"I'm not normally *that* lucky. But if I ask enough questions, sooner or later I usually get a lead."

"Well…"

"Is there a problem?"

"Just a minor one. Something else with Noah."

"Uh-huh?"

"You see, Larry and I don't think much of consultants. We've heard about too many cases of them causing more problems than they've solved. And

Noah's aware of how we feel, so he'll figure it's awfully strange that we'd suddenly decide to…

"But there's no reason for *you* to worry about that. Larry and I will come up with an explanation. Which gets us to the question of when you can start."

"Let's see," she said, glancing at her appointment book. "This is Wednesday and I'm tied up tomorrow. But I could meet with you and your partner on Friday morning."

"Sounds fine."

"Good. Then I'll need a small retainer now. And on Friday the two of you can fill me in on the details of these incidents.

"Plus, if you get together an organization chart, a list of your employees and copies of the latest annual reports, I'll review them on the weekend. And starting Monday, I'll be able to devote most of my time to you."

Since Robert seemed surprised, she added, "A lot of my work is for trial lawyers. But half of them spend their summers in the Hamptons, which makes July and August slow."

"Ah."

When he said nothing more, she began to grow anxious.

He looked worried that she might have given him the "slow summers" explanation to avoid the truth. And worried the truth was that she didn't have enough clients to earn a decent living.

However, since New Yorkers who concerned themselves about strangers were an endangered species, he was far more likely reconsidering the wisdom of hiring her—probably wondering if whoever had done the asking around for him had goofed, maybe suspecting she was *actually* readily available because she wasn't a particularly good P.I.

Uneasily, she pictured the anemic balance in her bank account. Then, to her relief, Robert Haine reached inside his suit jacket and produced a checkbook.

FOUR YEARS OF LIFE in squad cars had left Dana with absolutely no desire to ever drive in Manhattan again.

Besides, she liked walking, found that immersing herself in the constant rush of the city energized her. And when walking wasn't feasible she happily relied on cabs and public transit. She didn't need either, though, to get to Four Corners Imports.

Its head office was on the northern fringe of the Village, not much more than an easy stroll from her Chelsea apartment. And a pleasant one on a sunny July morning, even if the air was a bit too muggy for comfort.

After turning off Ninth onto West Thirteenth, she stopped to take her black pumps out of her briefcase and change into them from her sneakers. Then she tucked those away and started walking again—mentally reviewing the homework she'd done on the company's key players.

She'd learned, long ago, that checking out new clients often revealed interesting details they'd "forgotten" to mention. But in this instance she hadn't learned anything even remotely strange or startling.

Robert had begun his working career in sales. Then he'd met Larry Benzer—recently back from fighting in Vietnam and with a little money saved—and the two of them had established their own business.

Noah Haine, the nephew who'd joined the company a few years back, had initially been brought on board to orchestrate the process of taking it public.

With an MBA from Columbia and experience working for an investment banker, he'd been up on what had to be done to make Four Corners comply with all of the Securities and Exchange people's regulations.

As for the men's personal lives, Robert was well into his second marriage, no children from either. Larry and his wife had been together for almost twenty-five years. They had two sons and a daughter. Noah was single.

While a few more facts were parading through Dana's mind she reached her destination, which proved to be an old, but well-maintained, three-story brick office building.

Beyond the bar-protected glass of the front entrance she could see a wide, old-fashioned wooden staircase. To the right was a hallway, to the left a reception area.

It was accented with a variety of interesting-looking collectibles—undoubtedly examples of the sorts of things Four Corners imported. Between those and the numerous paintings on the walls, the space reminded her of a tiny gallery in a museum.

But when her gaze came to rest it wasn't on any of the objets d'art. It was on the tall, dark-haired man talking to the woman behind the desk.

His back was to the door, so she couldn't see his face. Given the set of his broad shoulders, though, combined with the relaxed way he was standing, she'd say he was the kind of man who felt comfortable in his own skin.

Hoping the humidity hadn't done too bad a number on her hair, she combed her fingers through it. Then she pressed the buzzer.

The receptionist glanced over, scrutinized her, then released the lock. Apparently, the woman had been expecting her. The man turned to see who had arrived.

When he did, she felt a quick internal tug—a feeling she so rarely had that she almost didn't recognize it for what it was. Instantaneous attraction. There was something about him…

She let herself study him for a moment, trying to determine exactly what it was, then finally decided it was a combination of things.

His eyes were the color of rich black coffee, his features strong and regular; his square jaw looked rock hard. All in all, it was hardly surprising that he'd started her pulse stuttering a little.

As she stepped inside he smiled at her—such a

high-beam smile she couldn't have stopped herself from smiling back if she'd tried. Then he glanced at her naked ring finger, and his apparent interest made her face grow warm.

Lord, how long had it been since she'd blushed? Certainly months. Possibly years.

"You must be Dana Mayfield," he said.

"Yes. And you must be...?"

The receptionist's phone began to ring.

"Noah Haine," he told her as the woman picked up. "Robert's nephew. I'll take you to him."

"Thanks."

"Most of our office space is on this floor," he said as she fell into step beside him. "Back there," he added, gesturing toward the wall behind the staircase.

She nodded, just able to hear the muffled sounds of people at work.

"But Robert and Larry hide out upstairs. They like to keep clear of the line of fire."

When he gave her a quick grin to say he was joking, she couldn't help thinking it was positively criminal that she'd have to ignore the pull she felt toward him.

New York was *not* a primo city for meeting eligible men. Not eligible men who rang *her* chimes, at any rate.

At thirty-one years of age, she'd been in precisely three serious relationships, none of which had been serious enough to lead to marriage.

And these days, all the single men she came in

contact with seemed to be either gay, work obsessed, or in critical need of therapy.

Given that, and adding in the fact she was...

She settled on *selective,* rejecting *picky*—a word her mother had been known to use. But semantics aside, the point was that Noah Haine was off-limits.

She firmly believed in never mixing pleasure with business. And even if that wasn't true she'd be careful around Noah. At least until she felt sure she could rule him out as a suspect.

After all, he *was* the director of finance. And one of the "incidents" had involved a batch of invoices that never reached the customers.

Blood might be thicker than water, but that didn't mean Noah-of-the-thousand-watt-smile couldn't be playing games.

That thought front and center in her mind, she managed to keep her eyes off him until they reached the second floor.

At the top of the stairs was a small waiting area. Beyond it stood an empty conference room, its door open, and to their left was a short corridor.

"The corner offices," Noah told her as they started toward them, "are my uncle's and Larry's.

"And this one in between belongs to Helen Rupert," he added, stopping outside its door.

He introduced Dana to the woman sitting behind the desk, then said, "Officially, Helen is Robert and Larry's executive assistant. In reality, she runs the company."

Helen, a plump woman in her fifties, laughed.

"That's only because I've been here forever," she said. "And I know where all the skeletons are buried."

Noah shot her a grin, then led Dana the rest of the way to Robert's office—where both the partners were waiting for her.

In contrast to Robert's refined appearance, Larry Benzer was a large man whom she'd have guessed would deal in sports equipment, or something of that sort, rather than collectibles.

He'd been a boxer in college, she recalled, thinking that even a brief check into someone's personal life usually turned up interesting bits of trivia. And he'd obviously kept in shape.

As he shook her hand, almost making her wince in the process, Robert said to Noah, "There's no reason you need to sit in on this. Larry and I are just going to give Dana an overview of the company."

The look that flickered across Noah's face said he suspected the older men were keeping something from him. And since his obvious guess would be that it was something to do with *her,* once he'd left she asked if he *had* thought it was strange that they'd hired a consultant.

"He was certainly surprised," Robert admitted. "But we came up with a pretty good story—said that while he was out of town Larry's wife began pushing the idea. Told him that she'd read an article about organizational designers and decided a good one could probably help pinpoint why we've been having problems."

"Noah's aware I haven't filled her in on our saboteur theory," Larry added. "If I did, she'd only be more concerned. So it would make sense to him that she's just thinking in terms of problems."

"I see," Dana said. "And when you talked to Noah? Did you get the impression that he really believed all it took was her suggesting—"

"You'd have to know Martha to understand," Larry interrupted. "Until a couple of years ago she worked with us. Actually, we hired her way back when, to help me with market development, and then I ended up marrying her.

"But that's beside the point. Which is that she still feels she's part of the company and...she's kind of headstrong."

Dana glanced at Robert in time to catch the hint of a weary smile. From that, she concluded Larry should have omitted the "kind of."

"When my wife sets her mind to something and doesn't get her way," he added, "she can drive people crazy."

"In other words," Robert said, "Noah won't be thinking it's *too* unrealistic that we'd go along with her."

Turning her gaze back to Larry, Dana said, "If she still feels she's part of the company, does she ever stop by, or..."

"Oh, sure. We have a condo in SoHo, so it's no

distance. And every now and then she has a marketing idea that she just can't wait to discuss.''

"I see," Dana said again, suspecting Martha Benzer was probably bored—and possibly regretted having left the company.

"Or she might want to go out for lunch on a day her friends are all busy," Larry was continuing. "And I'm better than staying home.''

"I'm sure you're *much* better," she said with a smile. "But I didn't make the reason for my question clear. I was wondering what would happen if she was here and ran into Noah. If he said something about *her* suggesting you hire me.''

"Oh, that's covered," Larry said. "I told her we were blaming you on her—as far as Noah and Helen and anyone else who might ask is concerned and...

"But I didn't mean *blaming* you. What I should have...well, the bottom line is, you don't have to worry about Martha.''

Dana didn't exactly understand what Martha knew and didn't know, but before she had a chance to ask anything more Larry was saying, "So, getting back to Noah, we said that we weren't hiring you *only* to make Martha happy. That we'd started thinking we might be too close to see clearly. And were hoping something might leap out at an outsider like you.''

"And what did Noah say?''

Robert shot Larry a look, then shrugged. "That it would have made more sense to hire a private eye.''

CHAPTER TWO

BACK IN HIS OWN OFFICE, Noah connected to the Internet and brought up his favorite search engine.

Seconds after he typed in *Dana Mayfield* a list of hits appeared. The third one took him by surprise. And sent him to Dana's Web site—where he sat staring at her biography.

A degree in business with a major in organizational design, plus more than five years' experience in the field. Quotes from satisfied clients followed the bio. And the photograph above the text was definitely a shot of the woman he'd left sitting in his uncle's office.

She was for real, then. Academically qualified and all.

That wasn't what he'd been expecting. In fact, he'd only decided to try her name on the off chance he'd learn who she *actually* was.

Because, since he'd looked her up in the phone book yesterday and found there was no listing, he'd been certain she was a fake.

After all, anyone who was self-employed wanted to make it easy for people to find them.

But now that he'd discovered this Web site...

He sat trying to figure out what reason she could have for not being in the book. Then it struck him that there wasn't an office address on the screen, only a phone number, and a possible explanation came to him.

Phone books contained street addresses. If she worked out of her apartment she *wouldn't* want to make it too easy for people to find her. Not to learn where she lived, at least.

Women in New York had to be careful about things like that. Especially, he imagined, women as good-looking as Dana Mayfield. And she *was* an exceptionally good-looking woman.

He let his gaze linger on her photograph.

Her eyes were as blue as a country sky and her dark hair was cut in a short, no-nonsense style—although the shaggy way it fell onto her forehead was decidedly sexy. As were her smooth, full lips and cute little nose.

He stared at the monitor for a few more seconds, thinking that picture looked so lifelike he could practically smell the tantalizing scent of her perfume.

Strange how you never knew when someone would suddenly walk into your life and...

Of course, in this instance there wouldn't be any "and." The last thing he needed was a distraction.

But if the timing wasn't so bad, and if she wasn't a potential problem, he just might be interested in her.

Just might?

He almost smiled, silently admitting there wasn't

much question about it. If he hadn't figured she was trouble, he'd probably have asked her to lunch about three seconds after she'd walked into the building.

He leaned back in his chair, thinking didn't this just beat all.

From the first moment he'd heard the name Dana Mayfield, he'd been almost positive that Robert and Larry were blowing smoke. That the woman they were telling him about was actually a P.I. Or that they'd taken their suspicions to the police, in which case she'd be an undercover cop.

And jeez he'd been angry, figuring they were lying to him.

Now, though, he realized it had been wasted emotion. He'd obviously jumped to the wrong conclusion.

Yet even with the proof of that right here in front of him, it was tough to believe. Because those two hiring a consultant was completely out of character.

Of course, if Martha Benzer had *seriously* gotten on their case about it…

But no. As big a pain as she could be, humoring her to this extent just didn't sound like the Robert and Larry *he* knew. So if they were going to hire someone, why *not* a P.I.?

The idea that they'd convinced themselves an OD consultant might help them with a problem like *theirs* seemed so remote…

It simply didn't add up.

He focused on Dana's photograph again—and began hoping to hell she wouldn't get in the way of what he was doing.

DANA HAD MOVED OUT of the house she'd grown up in and left Queens almost ten years ago. Yet every now and then, as she walked down the familiar street, she remembered how upset her parents had been at their "little girl's" announcement that she'd found an apartment.

"Manhattan isn't safe," her mother had repeated at least a dozen times.

"For heaven's sake, Mom," she'd finally said. "I'm a cop."

"I'm a cop, too, which is how we *know* it isn't safe," her father had muttered. "And you're barely through the academy."

"Dad, I'm twenty-two."

In his eyes, though, she'd been his baby. She probably always would be. His only child. And they were so close that...

That half the reason she'd joined the police force had been to follow in his footsteps, to make him proud of her. And he had been, until...

She told herself not to go there. The past was past; that chapter in her life over and done with.

Yet she still wished, for his sake if for no other reason, that she hadn't been forced to quit. Because even though he'd assured her a hundred times that he understood, she knew how badly she'd disappointed him.

She'd barely turned into the yard before he had the front door open and was heading down from the porch to greet her, saying, "Hey, my beautiful daughter's here. It must be Sunday."

"You think?" she said, stepping into his hug.

"Yeah, I think."

"We're in a rut, you know."

"Yeah, but it's a nice rut."

He draped his arm over her shoulders as they started for the house, pretending he wasn't even marginally interested in what she'd brought by way of groceries.

He was, though.

Jack Morancy liked his food, but he was *not* a handy man in the kitchen. So for the three years since her mother's death, most Sundays that he wasn't on duty he'd either come to Dana's apartment for dinner or she'd make the trip to Queens and they'd eat there.

Oh, sometimes he insisted on taking her out, but she really didn't mind doing the cooking.

Cops were notorious for eating badly, and even though she knew one healthy meal a week couldn't compensate for all the greasy fast food he had during his shifts, it couldn't hurt. Besides, they enjoyed the time together.

"Some of this should go in the fridge," she said once they were inside.

"Sure."

He followed her to the kitchen, and as she dug the

meat and low-cal sour cream out of the bag, asked, "So what happened in your world this week?"

"Well, I've got a new client. Or maybe I should say two. Business partners. I met with them on Friday and got going on some of the preliminary stuff yesterday."

"Good. Interesting case?"

"It definitely has the potential. They figure someone's sabotaging their company."

"Yeah? What sort of company?"

"They import collectibles. Art, small antiques. High-quality things."

"Oh? What's it called?"

"Four Corners Imports."

"Four corners of the world, huh? Good name. Big business?"

"Mmm...head office in New York and a few salespeople in L.A. But they outsource as much of the work as they can, so staff-wise they aren't all that large.

"At any rate, one of the partners, Robert Haine, takes care of acquiring most of the items. Spends half his life traveling, I gather. The other one, Larry Benzer, handles the majority of the marketing."

She closed the fridge door and turned to discover that her father was staring at her with a very strange expression.

"What's wrong?" she said.

There was a second's hesitation—or was she only imagining that?—before he said, "Nothing. I just...

So you've got one of them acquiring, the other one marketing. And while they're busy doing that who's running the show?''

"Basically, Robert's nephew. He's their director of finance.''

"Ah. A little nepotism.''

"Well, I imagine that helped get him hired, but my read is that he's good. And his area of responsibility seems to be a lot broader than his title suggests. He's really more a director of operations.''

Her father nodded, then said, "So tell me about the sabotage.''

"You want to hear the details?''

"Sure.''

"Well…'' She started to briefly fill him in on what Robert and Larry had told her, vaguely aware of feeling a touch uneasy.

Not that she was worried about confiding in him. Whenever she hit a snag she used him as a sounding board. And she knew anything she said would stay strictly between the two of them. But she'd suddenly gotten the sense he was a little *too* interested in this particular case.

She considered that for a moment, then decided the problem was more likely that she'd become overly suspicious. It routinely happened to cops and P.I.s.

Still, whether it was common or not, suspecting her own father wasn't simply curious about her work… Lord, that had to be really paranoid.

Forcing away her concern, she continued her summary of what had been happening at Four Corners.

Jack listened in silence—until she got to the part about the two shipping containers that had gone astray. When she said that their contents had been worth half a million dollars, he gave a low whistle.

It made her smile. "I told you they deal in quality stuff. At any rate, I have a call in to the police detective who caught the case. But I haven't heard back from him yet."

She returned to the details, finishing up by saying, "Larry Benzer's money is on one or more of the warehouse people. Because between the arson and those containers disappearing they're such obvious possibilities."

"The arson was definitely an inside job?"

"That's what the fire marshal decided. According to his report there was no sign of forced entry. So someone apparently had a key."

"Then you're probably looking at either a current or ex-employee."

"Exactly. And since all three of the full-time warehouse staff have been there for years, there's no disgruntled ex running around. So current would be the likely bet. But Robert Haine isn't convinced it *was* any of the warehouse guys."

"Oh? What does he think?"

"That their theory about a plot to drive down the share price is right. And he says none of the warehouse fellows is sophisticated enough to mastermind anything like that.''

''Have they both ruled out the idea that a competitor might be behind things?''

''I don't think so. At least not entirely. Someone *could* be paying off one of their employees. Or more than one. Or maybe *both* their theories are all wet.''

Her father nodded. ''Sounds like a case that might take a while to get a good feel for.''

''That's for sure. By the time they finished discussing everyone they thought the perp *could* be... Well, I was left thinking it might be almost anyone. I haven't even ruled out Robert's nephew.''

''The director of finance.''

She nodded.

''He a typical accountant type?''

When she couldn't help smiling, her father said, ''What's that about?''

''Nothing, really. Just that he's not *exactly* a typical accountant.''

Resisting the temptation to add that he wouldn't be even if someone forced him to wear wire-rimmed glasses and a pocket protector, she merely waited— fully expecting another question about Noah Haine.

Her mother would certainly have asked one. Her father, however, got straight back to business, saying ''What about those invoices that went missing? Any possibility of tying them to someone from the warehouse?''

''Surprisingly, yes. The best guess is that someone

lifted them while they were waiting to go out in the mail. And on paydays, one or another of the warehouse fellows stops by to pick up their checks.

"So it's conceivable one of them could have been responsible. Not likely, but conceivable."

Jack Morancy was silent for a minute, then said, "You didn't mention how these Four Corners people heard about you."

"You mean you don't think *everyone's* heard I'm the best P.I. in New York?"

He grinned. "Of course. Dumb of me to ask."

"Actually, someone on the force recommended me. But since Robert didn't do the checking around himself, he didn't know who."

That seemed to bring the conversation to an end, so she opened the fridge again and took out a pitcher of lemonade, saying, "Want to sit on the porch for a while?"

"Sure," her father told her. Then he smiled, but it wasn't his normal smile.

"Dad…is something bothering you?"

"Bothering me? No. Why?"

"I just thought…" She shrugged. "I guess I just thought wrong."

She hadn't, though. She was deep-down certain she hadn't.

DANA AND JACK MORANCY weren't quite finished dinner when her cell phone rang. Ted Tanaka, the

NYPD detective investigating the container theft, was finally getting back to her.

As it turned out, the investigation had stalled and he couldn't add much to what she already knew. But since she'd only given her father the bare bones of that—and since he sat watching her expectantly after she clicked off—she figured she'd better recap the conversation.

"He basically just repeated what Robert and Larry told me," she began. "What I was telling you earlier.

"Four Corners had six containers coming in on a cargo ship. It was Friday, the ship was late arriving and Stu Refkin, the warehouse manager, had plans for right after work. So he took off before the crew unloaded the shipment and left his two men to deal with it."

"By deal with it you mean…?"

"Move the containers from the pier into the warehouse."

"That only takes two people?"

"Two people and a lift truck. Anyway, they did that, then locked up and went home. But according to them, there were just four containers."

"Why wouldn't they know there were supposed to be six?"

She shrugged. "Stu says he *thinks* he mentioned the number—that he meant to but isn't entirely sure he did. They claim that, if so, they didn't hear him. And the one who signed the ship's delivery form barely looked at it. Didn't check how many it specified."

"Pretty sloppy."

"Yes, but I guess it's the sort of thing that becomes so routine…"

"Honey, nothing should ever be routine when you're talking half a million bucks. I'm surprised that guy still has his job."

"Well, the insurance company will pick up most of the loss. And I gather it was the first time anything like that ever happened.

"But I'm getting off track," she continued. "The important thing is that the company's men say there were only four containers while the ship's captain swears his crew unloaded six."

"So either he's lying or the warehouse guys are," her father said.

"Uh-huh. And the ship has a foreign registry and is long gone by now, which means Tanaka probably has all he's going to get from that end."

"This happened on a Friday," Jack said slowly.

"Yes. Then, come Monday, Stu Refkin arrived at work and discovered… Well, he got on the phone to Larry Benzer and Larry called the police."

Her father nodded. "In the meantime, if you assume all six containers *were* unloaded, the two warehouse guys would have had the entire weekend to dispose of them. And even a fence would have paid…

"But did this Tanaka tell you what *he* figures happened?"

"He thinks only four of them made it off the ship. A security guard patrols the piers, and moving containers out of the warehouse on a weekend would be unusual. So if he saw it happening he'd probably have questioned it. At the very least, he'd have made a note in his log.

"All in all, disposing of them would have been risky. So Tanaka's best guess is that the ship's captain intentionally shorted the delivery. But he also thinks the captain was in cahoots with someone at Four Corners."

"Someone like…?"

"Take your pick. Stu Refkin checked out and left the others in charge. And he'd probably know if they don't normally pay much attention when they sign receiving forms."

"Yeah, so the ship could have been *intentionally* late, letting this Refkin remove himself from the picture and…"

"But he's not our only contender. Tony Zicco, the guy who signed the delivery slip, hasn't always been Mr. Straight-and-Narrow.

"He ran with a bad crowd as a kid and eventually did a stretch for a B and E. It was his parole officer who got him the job at Four Corners."

"Now, *that's* an interesting wrinkle."

She nodded. "According to Robert, they've never had a single problem with Tony. But Larry figures… Well, I already told you what he thinks."

"That there's a rotten apple in the warehouse,"
Jack said.

"At least one. Maybe two or three."

"Yeah, they could all have been in on it. But, you
know, something isn't sitting right with me."

"What?"

"It's just *too* obvious. I mean *both* the arson and
this pointing toward the same people seems like over-
kill."

She nodded again, glad to hear her father's line of
reasoning coincided with hers. "And there's another
thing. They all offered to take lie detector tests."

That made him grin. "Sounds as if they watch too
many cop shows."

"Maybe. But Tanaka arranged for it. And according to the tests, none of them had anything to do with
either the arson *or* the theft of the containers."

"'Course...those things can be beaten."

"Uh-huh. So if it *was* only one of them involved,
and he managed to do that..."

Jack nodded, then said, "I think you were right.
This really *could* be an interesting case."

CHAPTER THREE

FIRST THING Monday morning Dana was at Four Corners once more, ready to step into her role as Dana *Mayfield.*

After she'd spent a few minutes asking Robert last-minute questions, he said he'd show her to the office she'd be using. Surprisingly, he led her over to the short hallway near the top of the stairs.

When she told him she hadn't expected to be on the "executive floor," he smiled.

"You'll have more privacy here," he said.

She knew that had to be true. *Tucked away and out of sight* would perfectly describe the location.

"As you'll see when you get the grand tour," he continued, "our office area downstairs is basically open concept."

"You're saying it's not quite ideal for someone doing undercover work."

He smiled again. "Exactly. I didn't think you'd want people looking over your shoulder.

"And these two offices are just sitting empty. Both Noah and our director of logistics, Chris Vidal, prefer to be on the main floor. They interact a lot with the rest of the staff, so being up here wouldn't work as well.

"That, by the way," he added, pointing toward a narrow back staircase, "will take you down to a hall that runs from the alley door to the main office area."

The stairs, she saw, also led to the top floor. When she asked what was up there, Robert said, "It's mostly dead storage. Filing cabinets full of old records and all sorts of other ghosts from the past thirty years."

She resisted the impulse to say that, considering costs in Manhattan, it was an incredibly expensive storage area.

Then she had the disconcerting sense Robert had ESP as he said, "We've got more room than we really need.

"Initially, we figured we'd use that space for additional employees as the business grew. But modern technology exploded, the work world changed and we didn't grow, people-wise, the way we'd anticipated."

Opening the office door, he ushered her inside. "Helen put some supplies in the desk and had that computer moved in. If there's anything else you need, just tell her."

"Thanks, I will."

She eyed the computer for a second, hoping it was loaded with software she knew, then turned her attention back to Robert.

He'd taken a couple of keys from his pocket and was saying, "These are for the door and the desk.

And I should show you this." He produced a sheet of paper and gave it to her along with the keys.

"After you left on Friday, I drafted a memo about you—made you sound as nonthreatening as I could."

She began skimming it. Addressed to "All Staff," it said that, in light of recent problems, he and Larry had hired an organizational design expert to look at the company's operations with fresh eyes.

It went on to say that while her findings might result in a few modifications to current practices, no changes would be made without the direct involvement of any employees affected.

"That was a good idea," she said once she'd finished reading. "People *do* tend to feel threatened by a stranger coming in and poking around."

He nodded. "I'd like to know how much anxiety you think there actually is. As well as have you keep me up-to-date on your progress. So let's set a regular time to touch base each day."

"Sure."

"Maybe late afternoon? Four-thirty or so? My office?"

"Fine."

She'd assumed from the beginning that this was more his project than Larry's, and by now she knew she was right. Which was perfectly okay.

She got positive vibes from him, but she couldn't say the same about his partner.

In fact, on a couple of occasions during their meeting last week, she'd had the impression that Larry had only agreed to hire an investigator because Robert was pushing the idea.

"Is there anything else we should discuss before you get started?" he said.

"I don't think so."

"Then I'll ask Helen to have Noah come up."

"Noah?"

"Uh-huh. Since we haven't told him you're really a P.I., there's no risk of his blowing your cover. Whereas both Larry and I have been known to say things without thinking.

"Besides, the obvious person to introduce you around is the one in charge of day-to-day operations."

"Ah. Good point."

There was no arguing with Robert's logic. But more than once over the weekend, a distracting image of Noah Haine had tiptoed through her mind. And she had a horrible suspicion that having the real thing at her side would prove a much bigger distraction than any image.

To stop herself from worrying about that, she sat down at the desk and jiggled the mouse, bringing the computer to life. Fortunately, it was loaded with Office—which was what she was used to.

She was just resisting the temptation to check whether Free Cell had been deleted when she heard footsteps in the hall. Her pulse began a funny little dance.

Firmly, she reminded herself she was an adult, not a teenager at the mercy of raging hormones. Despite that, all it took was Noah reaching her doorway and gracing her with one of his warm smiles to make her feel a distinct...

But it wasn't a feeling that had anything to do with raging hormones. It was merely a fresh flicker of awareness that he was an attractive man. And she had no difficulty ignoring flickers.

Unfortunately, she couldn't say the same about those darned smiles. She'd have to work at developing an immunity to them. Starting now.

When he closed her door and lowered himself into a chair, an unsettling sense that he'd just assumed control seized her—despite the fact that *she* was the one on the business side of the desk.

Then he smiled again and said, "Before we get going, how about filling me in on how you'll be approaching things. My uncle was pretty vague."

"Well, that's probably because I was pretty vague with *him*. OD isn't an exact science—as I'm sure you know. But generally speaking, I'll just start by getting people to talk about the company and their role in it. Then, depending on where that leads..."

Noah said nothing, simply sat watching her. She began to feel unsettled again.

He had a master's degree in business. A genuine one, as opposed to the one that existed on her trumped-up credentials. And that meant he could easily be far more knowledgeable about OD than she was.

If she inadvertently said anything dumb, would he pick up on it? She certainly hoped not.

"In this instance," she continued, telling herself she was doing fine thus far, "with Robert's memo referring to the fact that there've been specific problems, people will be expecting me to ask about them. So I will.

"Actually, since two of the *major* ones happened at the warehouse, I'd like to begin by talking with the staff there."

"You're going to make them nervous," he said quietly.

"I'll do my best not to."

THE FOUR CORNERS WAREHOUSE was only a few blocks from its head office, on one of the multitude of piers reaching out into the Hudson River.

Noah opened the door and ushered Dana inside, thinking—not for the first time—that the work crew the insurance company had sent in had done wonders.

"Seeing this place now," he said, "you wouldn't believe what a charred disaster it was after the fire. Just about everything being stored had suffered either smoke or water damage. And the air was so acrid you could feel it searing your lungs."

She nodded. "I've been in burned-out buildings."

"Oh?"

Wondering why she would have been, he waited for her to elaborate.

She didn't, merely glanced around, then said,

"How soon after they had the fire out were you in here?"

"Well, it was out by about two in the morning. The fire marshal didn't let me have a look until after dawn, though. And even then it barely qualified as a look because they had it taped off as a crime scene."

"But you're saying you were here most of the night?"

He nodded. "I came as soon as I heard we had trouble. One of the administrators is always on call, either Robert, Larry or me. And it was me that night."

"Is that unusual? Having an admin person on call in this type of business?"

He shrugged. "Every so often a problem comes up after hours. Five o'clock here is only two in L.A.

"Fortunately, though, our problems usually have to do with a missed delivery or that sort of thing. Not a fire."

When she smiled, his heart gave a little thud against his ribs.

He warned himself to watch out.

Nothing had changed over the weekend. This *still* wasn't a good time for him to get interested in a woman. Particularly not *this* woman.

"Who discovered the fire?" she was saying. "Not that it has anything to do with my job here, but you've got me curious."

"Well, a security company patrols this pier and the ones closest to it."

Her nod showed she'd already known that, making

him think Robert and Larry must have done a thorough job of filling her in.

"Their guard called 911," he continued. "Then, once the fire trucks were on their way, he contacted our answering service. And they phoned me.

"I got here not long after the firefighters. I just live over in Murray Hill."

She started to ask another question, stopping as Stu Refkin appeared from behind a crate in the back.

He eyed them for a moment, then raked his fingers through his graying hair and started across the floor.

"This is our warehouse manager," Noah said as he reached them. "Stu Refkin, Dana Mayfield."

The man extended his hand, looking far from happy.

"We got the boss's memo about you," he said. "But I didn't expect to see you so soon.

"No offense," he quickly added.

She smiled. "None taken."

"Good. Then let me go get my men. I know they'll want to meet you."

Noah didn't buy that for a second. As he'd warned Dana earlier, she was going to make all three of these fellows nervous.

A couple of minutes passed before Stu arrived back with Tony Zicco and Paul Coulter in tow.

Tony had dark hair, Paul's was a sandy color, but there were more similarities than differences in their appearances. Both were early forties, a shade under six feet tall, with muscular builds that indicated they did physically demanding work.

After going through introductions a second time, Noah made a bit of small talk. Then his cellular rang, giving him an excuse to leave the four of them on their own.

It was Helen calling, with a question that only took a minute to answer. But when he clicked off, rather than rejoining the others, he wandered over to the window beside the door and stood, ostensibly staring out at the murky water of the Hudson.

In reality, he was watching the little group's reflection in the glass, absently adding up how many years—in total—the three men had worked at Four Corners.

Stu had been with the company since start-up, for the first ten years as one of the warehouse grunt men, for the past twenty as manager.

Tony and Paul hadn't been around forever but both were long-term employees.

He'd had a careful look through their files after the container incident, so he knew Paul had been around for close to eighteen years. And Tony had come on board about three years later—almost straight out of prison.

But he'd always been a good employee. Surely he wouldn't go bad again after so much time had passed.

Or would he?

Maybe he'd needed big money for some reason and…

Telling himself speculation about that sort of thing was a waste of time, Noah focused on the reflection once more.

All three men looked worried, but they'd be a lot more so if they'd overheard some of the discussions he'd had with Robert and Larry. If they knew Larry kept harping on the point that lie detector tests weren't foolproof, and insisting at least one of the warehouse people had to be part of what he'd taken to calling "the conspiracy"...

However, surely anyone who gave his conclusion much thought would question it. Because none of these three seemed like the sort who'd get involved in a master plan to cause the company grief.

So wouldn't most people figure Larry was probably wrong? That someone *else* had tried to burn the place down?

And even though Tony had made a major-league slipup when he'd signed for those containers, that was a far cry from conspiring with the ship's captain to steal a couple of them.

Noah let his gaze drift to Dana's reflection, wondering what impression she was forming of these guys. Did she think one of them could be...

Of course, Robert had said he'd underplayed the sabotage angle with her. That he'd merely mentioned they thought it was *possible* someone was intentionally causing their problems.

Still, it would have occurred to her that the arsonist might be an employee.

He watched her for a few more seconds. And even though looking at her told him nothing about what was going on in her head, it was plain to see that those smiles she kept flashing weren't getting her anywhere. She was still making the men uneasy.

Not only that...

Studying her image in the glass, he silently admitted she was making him uneasy, as well. Because something about her didn't ring true.

He wasn't entirely sure why he had that feeling, although the fact they were here in the warehouse accounted for part of it.

Based on what *he* knew about the way consultants worked, she should have had him introduce her to the office staff first. Made her way over here sometime after that.

So even though she'd given him a plausible reason for where she wanted to begin, the fact remained that she wasn't behaving like a typical consultant.

And then there was her response when he'd asked her how she'd be proceeding.

She'd start by talking to people and see where it led. That was the extent of what she'd said—and it had set off a minor alarm in his brain.

People who specialized in organizational design, the ones he'd known in university, at least, were always more than eager to talk about the guiding principles they followed.

As Dana herself had said, OD wasn't an exact science. Which seemed to make its practitioners feel they should work at convincing everyone they met that it deserved respect.

Not Dana, though.

He had the distinct feeling that the less she discussed the finer points of her profession the happier she'd be. Which had him thinking…

Regardless of her Web site, he was back to suspecting his uncle and Larry had lied to him, that she was either a cop or a P.I.

Maybe it wasn't much more than a hunch, but he'd learned not to ignore his hunches. And if he was right about her, why were those two keeping him in the dark?

Only one obvious answer came to mind and he *really* didn't like it.

Larry might keep talking about how he suspected the warehouse guys. But when he was alone with Robert he had to be suggesting Noah could be behind things.

The thought his uncle would even consider that was… Yet what other explanation made sense?

Hell, that was probably the *real* reason Robert had him playing tour guide for Dana. It would give her time with him. Time to figure out if he was the guilty one.

Gazing at her reflection again, he decided he had to establish whether she was a phony or not—and fast.

As the old saying went, forewarned was forearmed,

and it had occurred to him, right off the bat, that she might get in the way of what he was doing.

Now he was thinking that, unless his hunch was wrong, there was little doubt she *would*.

Casually, he turned from the window and started toward the others.

When Dana noticed him coming, he said, "You're going to be here for a while, so I'll head back. Do some work until you need me again."

"Well...fine."

"My office is to the right of the front door. Just down the hall."

"Fine," she said again.

After nodding to the three men, he strode out of the warehouse and up the pier to West Street.

Ten minutes later he was at his computer, reading through those quotes from "clients" on Dana's Web site and thinking it was strange that she wouldn't have included the names of the client companies.

Or maybe it *wasn't* strange. If they weren't for real, they didn't *have* names.

He reached for his phone and dialed the number on the screen, then listened to her voice telling him he'd reached the office of Dana Mayfield, organizational design consultant, and asking him to leave a message.

He hung up, not even marginally convinced his hunch was wrong, then went into a database that gave him the options of searching the city by either address, zip or phone number.

When he typed in her number, there was no hit.

Yet it was obviously assigned, which meant she'd intentionally had it blocked.

A blocked *business* number? That made him even more suspicious. But how was he going to find out for *sure* if his suspicions were right? Follow her home?

No, that didn't strike him as much of a plan. He'd be smarter to try charm. Befriend her. Get her talking about herself. Then catch her off guard.

Uh-huh, that was a far better idea.

Except that he was kind of rusty in the charm department. He'd been so busy around here lately that his social life was nothing but a faded memory.

Glancing at Dana's photo once more, he told himself not to worry about the rust. Being charming to a woman who looked like her wouldn't be tough. No matter how high the likelihood that she was a phony.

On the other hand, he'd never been a good actor. So if she *was* a detective...

Well, he'd just have to be careful. And hope for the best.

IT WAS QUARTER TO TWELVE before Dana got back from the warehouse, and she headed straight down the hall next to the front entrance.

The door of the first office along it was closed, but its nameplate told her it belonged to Chris Vidal, director of logistics.

Noah's was the one farther along—the corner

one—and he was at his desk. Seeing her, he shot her another of his devastating smiles.

It reminded her she'd decided to work on developing immunity to them. Although she might not work too hard.

After all, she didn't have a rule about mixing pleasure with *ex*-business. So once her job here was through…

Telling herself to leave contemplating that until she was a lot closer to its *being* through—not to mention until she was absolutely *certain* Noah was one of the good guys—she said, "I just wanted to check that you'll still be available later."

"Sure. How did it go at the warehouse?"

"Not badly."

"Good. Hey, it's almost noon," he added, glancing at his watch. "There's a deli on Gansevoort that isn't bad. Want to try it?"

"Thanks, but I've got to write myself some notes about this morning. And if I don't do it now I'll forget half of what I heard."

"I can wait a bit," he said casually.

"Well…actually, I'm going to skip lunch."

"Ah." He hesitated, then said, "Dana, if I just gave you the impression that… I *was* only talking about lunch.

"No, wait, I think that came out wrong. I didn't mean to sound as if I might not be interested in…"

He shook his head and grinned. "I should probably stop before I get in even deeper. But what I was trying to say is that I didn't have a hidden agenda. I just figured you might like someone to eat with.''

''Well, I appreciate that. And you *didn't* give me the wrong impression. I'd decided to skip lunch before you said a word. I ended up spending a lot more time with Stu Refkin than I'd expected.''

''Ah,'' he said a second time. ''Okay, then. I'll be back by one, so whatever works after that...''

''Fine. See you later.''

Starting for the stairs, she felt as if a little candle were glowing inside her. When a man stumbled all over his words talking to a woman...

Of course, she'd already been pretty sure the attraction was mutual, but ''certain'' was better than ''pretty sure.'' Much better.

CHAPTER FOUR

THE SECOND FLOOR SEEMED deserted when Dana reached it, which was just as well. She had a feeling that Helen Rupert was a chatty woman—nice, but chatty. And she really did have to get those notes written.

Whenever feasible, she avoided using tape recorders. They often made people reluctant to speak freely. But the downside to relying on her memory was how quickly things began slipping from her mind.

She reached her own office and opened the door, thinking she should tell someone that the lock wasn't working. Then she stepped inside and her brain shifted gears.

On the surface of her desk, to the left of the computer, lay a white, letter-size envelope.

Two disposable latex gloves were precisely positioned next to it, one on either side.

Untouched by human hands? No fingerprints? Was that their message?

Odds were, she decided. And odds also were that whoever had left this for her was a tad on the weird side.

She picked up the envelope, opened its unsealed

flap—absently thinking no fingerprints *or* traces of saliva—and removed the single sheet of paper. She silently read the computer-printed message.

I know who you really are. And I know who set the warehouse fire. It was Noah Haine.

Her mouth a little dry and her heartbeat a little fast, she sat down.

What the hell was this? A joke?

If so, it wasn't a funny one.

And who had left it here, anyway?

She had no way of knowing, of course. Using the back stairs, anyone could have come up without being seen.

Or maybe one of those ghosts Robert had mentioned had snuck down from the third floor.

But where had that thought come from? Was her subconscious trying to creep her out?

Reminding herself she didn't believe in ghosts, she gazed at the words again.

I know who you really are.

Okay. That could mean exactly what it said, or could merely mean that someone *suspected* she wasn't an OD consultant.

And I know who set the warehouse fire.

Possibly. But if true, why hadn't this person told the fire marshal? And why tell her?

It was Noah Haine. Noah Haine, the first Four Corners person on the scene after the fire.

But what about before it?

She exhaled slowly. If she was going to figure out any answers to her questions, she had to think calmly and logically.

The arson had been an inside job, the arsonist someone with a key to the warehouse.

Or someone with a master key, her internal voice of reason pointed out.

She'd asked Robert about master keys, so she knew a single one opened both this building's doors and the warehouse's. And the three people with masters were Robert, Larry and Noah.

Robert and Larry, who had hired a P.I. Noah, who'd had no part in the decision—who didn't even know she *was* an investigator. But it was a huge leap from that to the possibility he was the arsonist.

The question of the moment was *how* huge?

He'd said he'd been home when the service called him. That, however, left some vital information missing.

How long between when the fire was started and when the security guard discovered it? How long after that before he called the service? Then before it called Noah?

More than enough time for him to get from the warehouse to Murray Hill, she'd bet.

Lord, when she'd told herself those missing invoices meant she couldn't rule him out too fast she'd only been about three percent serious. Now, though…

Yet what did she really have?

She stared at the note again, aware it was most likely the work of…

Never mind someone a tad on the weird side, it could be the work of a total nutcase. Could have absolutely no basis in reality. *Probably* had absolutely no basis in reality.

But what if it did?

Doing her best to ignore the dull buzz that had started in her head, she began cobbling together some of the pieces that *might* be relevant.

If she assumed that the theory Robert favored was right, that the problems were all part of a plan to drive down the company's share price, then whoever was behind it would have to be both smart and circumspect. Stock manipulation was illegal.

So who would know how to pull off that sort of thing with minimum risk of ending up in jail?

There was an only too obvious answer. The man who'd been brought into Four Corners specifically to help take it public—because he knew all the ins and outs of the Securities and Exchange Commission.

FIFTEEN MINUTES BEFORE Dana's first scheduled "touching base" meeting with Robert Haine, she hit the print key on her computer.

While the notes she'd just finished were turning into hard copy, she dug her cellular from her briefcase and used it to check her Dana Morancy, P.I., voice mail.

Getting that note was going to make her even more

careful than usual. And *careful* included not using a Four Corners phone to call her real self.

For all she knew, her note writer had a quick and easy way of checking the company's phone records.

There were a few messages for her, all business related except for a friend suggesting they get tickets to a new off-Broadway show. None was from anyone in urgent need of an investigator.

That, however, was just as well.

She'd never been *desperate* for clients, not even in the beginning. But she was rarely awash with them. So she didn't like having to turn any away. And if today was a good indicator, this job could take a while.

After making the one return call she couldn't leave for later, she stuck the freshly printed notes, along with the ones she'd put together at lunchtime, into a file folder—thinking she'd better try to get Robert more interested in hearing about her morning than her afternoon. *It* was basically a blur.

As promised, Noah had introduced her to some of the head office employees. But she'd done a poor job of concentrating on what they'd said to her. Her attention had been constantly wandering.

Every few seconds she'd caught herself watching Noah out of the corner of her eye, as if she'd actually believed she might see something that would tell her whether or not he was the arsonist.

What had she figured? That he'd set a desk on fire? Hardly a realistic scenario.

Shaking her head, she silently admitted her behavior this afternoon had *not* been rational. Especially not considering that by the time…

Well, the arson note had really gotten her mind spinning, and at first she'd been seriously wondering if Noah *was* the one.

But by the time he'd taken her around, she'd had long enough to have given the situation a lot more thought. And she'd reached the conclusion that, despite the things that seemingly pointed in the direction of his guilt, he really wasn't a very likely suspect.

She absently tapped her finger against the folder, still convinced she'd ultimately arrived at the *right* conclusion.

After all, nobody with half a brain would give much credence to an anonymous note accompanied by a pair of latex gloves. So she'd be awfully naive to believe Noah was the arsonist just because the writer said so.

In addition, Noah was far from the only person in New York who could be working a stock manipulation scheme. For that matter, there might not even be one. Until someone proved it true, a theory was nothing more than a theory.

Then there was the fact that Noah was Robert's nephew. Plus, he had a terrific job here and…

But what if he wanted more than that? What if he wanted to make a truckload of easy money? Retire to some tropical island by the time he hit forty.

No. She sincerely didn't think that was the case.

She was a good judge of character and she simply couldn't see... Of course, she barely knew him. And her judgment wasn't infallible.

She mentally shook her head, aware she'd feel far better if she was *certain* he couldn't have started that fire.

Conceivably, though, he could have. "Home alone" wasn't much of an alibi.

Of course, maybe he hadn't been alone. There might have been someone with him.

A woman.

As those words whispered in her mind she felt a twinge of... She wasn't sure exactly *what* it was, but if anyone had been with him that would be good. Then she *could* be certain he was innocent. So it was too bad that just coming straight out and asking him wasn't an option.

But he'd know that real OD consultants didn't try to identify arsonists on the side, and she didn't want to blow her cover—the way she'd almost done this morning.

After she'd said she'd been in burned-out buildings he'd clearly been curious about the circumstances. And if she hadn't caught herself before saying it was back when she'd been on the job...

Well, actually, avoiding telling people she was an ex-cop was more a habit than a question of catching herself.

Oh, she routinely told prospective clients. She figured it gave her more credibility. But when it came to other people she tended to keep quiet.

Too often, if she didn't, it led to questions about why she'd left the force. And in this case, it would *really* have led to questions.

Noah would have thought that cop to OD consultant was a very strange career path.

Telling herself to stop thinking about Noah Haine, she rose and picked up the file folder. Then she double-checked that the desk drawers were locked.

Until she decided what, if anything, to do about the arson note, she didn't want anyone seeing it. And nobody would with it hidden at the bottom of her briefcase and locked up tight.

WHEN DANA PAUSED in Robert's office doorway, he rose from his desk and motioned her toward the conversation area in the corner, saying, "How did your day go?"

She manufactured a smile. "If you mean have I figured out who your saboteur is, the answer's no."

He laughed. "But you *have* narrowed it down to just a couple of suspects, right? So by this time tomorrow…"

"Don't I wish. I haven't even met half your staff yet. I basically spent the morning at the warehouse. And this afternoon Noah introduced me to some of the people here, but I reached the limit of what I could absorb pretty fast."

"Let's hear about the morning, then."

Good. They were where she wanted to be, topic-wise.

"Well," she began, "I talked with all three men for a bit, and made a point of mentioning that I'll be chatting with every employee in the company. So they know they're not being singled out. Then I sat down with Stu Refkin and suggested he tell me about a typical day.

"Rather than do that, though, he cut straight to the chase and said he assumed I knew about the arson and the lost containers. Then we went from there."

"I'm not surprised," Robert told her. "Stu's always direct."

She smiled again—more genuinely this time. Robert had a knack for putting people at ease.

"He couldn't have been *more* direct," she said. "He began by saying that neither he nor his men have a clue who set the fire. As for the containers, he admitted there's no excuse for what happened. Said Tony should have checked the number unloaded against the delivery form. Period.

"I don't mean Stu was trying to distance himself from the blame," she continued. "Actually, it was quite the opposite.

"He said there'd have *been* no problem if he'd waited around until the ship arrived. And that he would have if he hadn't had plans."

"Right. He's been saying that from the beginning. In fact, none of them has changed his story in the

slightest. Whether they've been talking to me, the police, the insurance adjuster…''

''I should ask about something,'' Dana said when
he paused.

He waited.

''You said 'whether they've been talking to *you*.'''

''Uh-huh?''

''Did they talk to Larry and Noah, too?''

''Not that I'm aware of. I was the one who went
over what happened with them.''

''But why would it have been you rather than
Noah? I mean, if he's in charge of the day-to-day
operations…''

''You know something?''

''What?''

''For a *fake* OD consultant you're pretty good. The
administrative lines here *are* more blurry than they
should be.''

''I was wondering about that.''

''Yeah, well, until we hired Noah, Larry and I basically ran things by the seat of our pants. I don't
remember if I mentioned this before, but the financial
side of the business was always a mess—because neither of us is good with balance sheets and whatever.

''When it came to other things, whoever heard
about a problem first would take care of it.

''And as they say, old habits die hard. So you have
that, plus the fact the staff—especially the old-
timers—have always come to Larry or me, and…

"Well, they sometimes still do, and then we tend to jump on things we *should* leave to Noah."

She nodded. She didn't need to be a *real* expert to know people didn't change their behavior patterns easily.

"But getting back to what I said about how consistent the fellows' stories have been," Robert continued, "is it common for people to slip up and contradict themselves? If one of them *did* have something to do with either incident…"

"It happens. More often in the movies than in real life, though."

"Stu's worked here for thirty years," Robert said quietly.

"I know."

"And he's a good manager. I can't recall the last time we had a serious problem in the warehouse— before all this *stuff* started happening."

Fleetingly, she recalled her father saying he was surprised the warehouse people hadn't been fired. They probably would have been in most companies.

But thirty years and no problems obviously counted for something with Robert—which made her like him even more than she already did.

Glancing at her notes, she checked to see what else she should mention, then said, "Stu made sure I knew all three of them had taken lie detector tests. And that I'd been told they'd *asked* to take them."

There were a few seconds of silence then, before Robert said, "Do you figure there's *any* chance Stu was in on what happened? That he knew ahead of time the delivery was going to be short? That he and the captain…''

''I don't think there's *much* chance. Although one thing bothered me.''

''Oh?''

''The plans he had. The reason he didn't wait for the ship to arrive.''

''He'd promised to meet his wife. She wanted to look at some furniture.''

Dana nodded. ''I already knew that's what he told Detective Tanaka. But when he told *me* I had a feeling he was lying.''

''Oh?'' Robert said again, more slowly this time. ''Did Tanaka get that impression, too?''

''If he did, he didn't mention it. But I'm good at knowing when people aren't telling the truth. My father's a cop. He taught me what to look for when I was just a kid, so I've had years of practice. And I don't think Stu was meeting his wife.''

''Then what *do* you think?''

''That if anyone asked her she'd back him up. The names of the stores they went to would probably be on the tip of her tongue. But it wouldn't prove anything.''

Robert gazed at her, looking decidedly unhappy. Finally, he said, ''So, assuming you're right, he just doesn't want anyone to know what he was *really* doing that evening.''

"Exactly. Which is why I'm not entirely ready to write him off as innocent.

"On the other hand, I give a lot of weight to the results of those lie detector tests. It isn't easy to beat them."

"Only Larry seems to figure it is," Robert said.

NOAH WAS *NOT* A MAN WHO lurked. Yet he knew that was the only word to describe what he was doing at the moment.

Virtually everyone else had left for home by now, but here he was, standing partway between his office and the front door, lurking.

Glancing at his watch, he wondered how much longer that woman would be spending with his uncle.

It didn't matter, though. However long it was he'd still be here. He wanted the answers to some questions and he intended to get them.

He paced to his office door, then back down the hall again, almost banging into Chris Vidal, their director of logistics, who was coming out of the main office area.

"On your way home?" Chris asked.

"Shortly. I'm just waiting to catch Robert," he added when the other man obviously expected more.

"Oh, well, if you've got a minute, tell me what you think of these new rates Intercoastal Vans has in mind."

Chris dug a couple of sheets from the folder he was carrying. "They've changed the formula for their weight, volume and distance calculations, and I don't think it'll be to our benefit. But the explanation's so damned convoluted..."

Noah skimmed the pages, hoping Dana didn't make good her escape while Chris had him captured.

"Yeah," he said when he was done. "I'd say you're right. We'd really get nailed on some of those overweight charges."

"I'll give them a call in the morning, then," Chris said, sticking the papers back into his folder. "Talk to them about a guaranteed max."

"Good idea."

Noah watched Chris disappear into his office, then went back to thinking about Dana—and assuring himself he wasn't paranoid. There was no way he'd merely imagined that she'd been covertly watching him this afternoon.

Oh, she'd been very subtle about it. If he hadn't found himself gazing at *her* so frequently, he'd never have realized what she was doing.

But he'd introduce her to someone, and a few minutes later he'd see that she was less interested in the conversation than in keeping track of him.

And it sure wasn't because she found him wildly attractive. She hadn't been looking at him with stars in her eyes. What he'd seen in them was suspicion.

Man, oh, man, she was *not* what she was pretending to be. He had no lingering doubts on that score, was entirely back to being convinced she was either a cop or a P.I.

And he had a horrible feeling his worst fear about why she'd actually been hired was bang on.

Larry had convinced Robert that his own nephew could be behind the sabotage. So they had Ms. Who-ever-she-really-was in here to check him out.

Looking at his watch again, he reminded himself that all he had to do was learn where she lived. Once he knew that, getting her real identity should be easy.

A doorman might be persuaded to talk, if there was one. Failing that, he'd go back to his NYC database.

She might have avoided any link between her Dana Mayfield, OD consultant, phone number and other in-formation, but he'd be able to get a list of the occu-pants in her building. Then, by process of elimina-tion...

Of course, if it was a large place, that could present quite a challenge. But he'd do whatever he had to, and after he knew for sure...

He put the brakes on his thoughts. He was going to take this one step at a time and he didn't have much hard information yet.

At this point, the only thing he was certain of was that she lived *somewhere* in Manhattan. And that it couldn't be too far from here, because she'd men-tioned that she'd walked to the office this morning.

So, first, he'd offer her a ride home. That had to be worth a try, even though he expected she'd turn him down.

If she wasn't who she claimed to be, she wouldn't

want him knowing a thing about the *real* her. And that, of course, included where she lived.

But if she *didn't* say no... Would that mean he was totally wrong about this?

Uh-uh. He simply couldn't believe he was.

He heard the faint noise of footsteps on the stairs and waited, not breathing, until the sounds reached the bottom. Then he strode to the end of the hall and did his best to look surprised when he saw her.

"Working late your first day?" he said.

She smiled. "Trying to impress people."

Opening the door, he ushered her ahead of him, saying, "Which way do you go?"

"North."

"Ah, me, too."

"Oh?"

"I'm not on my way home," he quickly added, remembering he'd told her where he lived. And Murray Hill was more east than north.

"But why don't I give you a ride. My car's parked just behind the building."

"Well, thanks, but I'd rather walk." She pointed to the sneakers she'd changed into. "I'm all set."

He nodded. "You're sure I can't tempt you, though? It's still awfully hot."

"Even so, walking's the only exercise I get."

"Ah. Then I guess I'll see you tomorrow."

"I guess." She gave him another smile before heading down the street, leaving him muttering.

Now what did he do? Follow her?

He wasn't a man who did *that,* either. And when the idea had occurred to him, earlier, he'd rejected it. But how else was he going to find out what he wanted to know?

He took a few steps toward the narrow passage that led back to the alley—then stopped.

It was rush hour. She'd be walking faster than the traffic was moving.

On the other hand, his car had air, he was wearing a suit and the temperature had to be in the nineties.

But the bottom line was that he didn't want to lose her. So he removed his jacket, slung it over his shoulder and started off after her on foot.

CHAPTER FIVE

THE FRIEND DANA HAD SUBLET her apartment from always used to describe the building as old but well maintained.

It was a phrase she recalled every time she was standing on the front steps, unable to get the door unlocked on the first try. Or the second.

Not that this was a *bad* building. Its Chelsea location allowed her to walk just about everywhere. And with only three stories, it was small enough that her neighbors weren't just anonymous faces. Most of them were even pleasant.

But no matter how many times the super "worked his magic," as he liked to put it, this lock began acting up again after only a week or two.

If a mugger ever came along while she was struggling with it…

The thought prompted her to carefully scan the street.

The cars that were parked nose-to-bumper along the curb all seemed empty. There were a couple of men carrying briefcases, on their way home from work, a woman walking an oversize dog, and the resident dealer slouched against the building two down from hers, talking on a cell phone while he waited for his next customer.

Nothing at all out of the ordinary, which meant her intuition must be playing tricks.

Twice, on the way home, it had warned her to look back the way she'd come. But when she had, she hadn't spotted anyone following her.

So what had given her the creepy feeling that someone was?

She'd probably never know, and there wasn't much use in worrying about it when she had a more pressing concern.

She eased the key into its slot once more, thinking how ironic it was that she now had both a door at Four Corners she couldn't *lock* and one at home she couldn't *un*lock.

She gave the key a little jiggle before turning it this time, and voilà! Her effort was rewarded with a solid click.

Once in the foyer, she carefully closed the door behind her. Then she passed by the elevator, which was too unreliable to be trusted, and climbed the stairs to her third-floor apartment.

Inside, Dr. Watson greeted her with his customary enthusiasm, meowing loudly while trying to wrap his body entirely around her ankles.

"Hi, Doc," she said, sliding the dead bolts before setting down her briefcase and picking him up for a cuddle.

The cat, and his name, had come courtesy of her

father. One winter night, he and his partner had been checking out a possible break-in on Delancey. They'd returned to the squad car to find Dr. Watson huddled near it, a half-starved kitten that would have lost his ears to frostbite if they hadn't taken him straight to a twenty-four-hour veterinary clinic.

That had been only a few weeks after she'd gotten her P.I. license, and her father had brought Doc straight from the clinic to her, saying that since she'd decided she wanted to be Sherlock Holmes she'd better have a Dr. Watson.

"We'll do dinner in a while," she assured him, putting him back down. "It's early yet.

"Fish Delight. Worth waiting for," she promised as he impatiently twitched his tail.

When she headed into the bedroom, both answering machine lights were blinking. She looked at the caller ID display on the Dana Mayfield, OD consultant, line first.

One call, and it had come from Four Corners. *Someone* there had been checking up on her.

Feeling a little unsettled, she pressed the play button. There was no message, just a hang up. But somebody was clearly suspicious—at the very least. And the obvious suspect was her note writer.

After listening to the message on her personal line, from her friend Mary, she made a mental note to phone back later. Then she booted the computer to check her e-mail.

The room was large enough that—for the initial

few months of her P.I. career—she'd used one corner of it as her office.

She could hardly meet with clients in her bedroom, though, which meant that as soon as she'd acquired a few of them she'd had to rent a *real* office. But she still kept the older of her computers here to use when she had work to do in the evenings.

No interesting mail came in, so she wandered back to the front hall, retrieved her briefcase and carried it into the living room—where she sank onto the couch, toying with the idea of calling her dad and asking what *he* made of the arson note.

Thinking she'd have another look at it before deciding, she opened the case to dig it out. But she didn't get to the digging part.

Tucked into one of her black pumps was a second white envelope. Neatly wrapped around it was another pair of disposable latex gloves. Just in case she had a short memory, she assumed uneasily.

Doing her best to ignore the apprehension curling in her stomach, she reached for the envelope—already mentally reviewing her final few minutes at Four Corners.

After she'd gone from Robert's office to her own, she'd unlocked her desk drawer, removed the briefcase and changed from her dress shoes to her sneakers. Then she'd put the shoes into the case…and left it sitting on her desk while she went to the washroom.

She *had* shut her office door, though. And she hadn't been gone long.

But it had been long enough for someone to leave this for her.

Her pulse beating a bit faster than normal, she took out the sheet of paper that was inside the envelope.

You had your chance. You had today. But you didn't get anywhere, did you.

Not too smart. And I don't like people who aren't smart. So don't come back. Ever. If you do I'll make you sorry. Dead sorry.

Now her pulse was beating *way* faster than normal. She'd never had a direct threat like this before and she couldn't deny it made her anxious.

She took a deep breath and exhaled slowly, assuring herself that she was perfectly safe in her apartment.

As far as she knew, the other tenants were as careful as she was about closing the front door. That meant nobody who didn't live here could get in without being buzzed.

Although there was always the risk…

But she could make herself crazy by worrying about every risk in the world, so she focused on the message again.

She'd had her chance to what?

She doubted the writer meant her chance to sort out the company's organizational design problems. The line was far more likely related to the one in the arson note that said *I know who you really are.*

Wondering whether he actually did, she searched through the bottom of her briefcase and unearthed the first note. Maybe looking at the two of them together would spark a thought.

When she set them side by side the only thought she had was that they'd been printed on the same printer—which didn't exactly qualify as a stroke of genius. They'd hardly be the creations of two different warped minds.

But the printer had to be her starting point.

Assuming it was at Four Corners, and that she could get her hands on the right print sample, the one that would determine which printer it was... But she couldn't do anything about that tonight.

Well, actually, there was *one* thing, because she'd put Robert's "All Staff" memo about her into the side pocket of her briefcase.

She took it out and compared it with the notes, not even marginally surprised to see the print was different. She hadn't expected to discover the anonymous notes had come from the computer sitting on his desk.

Of course, Helen might have typed the "all staffer." But whether it had been Robert's machine or hers, this print *wasn't* a match.

Absently pushing her hair back from her face, Dana closed her eyes and took a long, slow breath.

Occasionally, she found that visualizing a scene let her recall something she hadn't been aware of while it had actually unfolded. So she began to imagine she was just coming out of Robert's office.

It was well past five; all was quiet on the second floor. Both Larry's office door and Helen Rupert's were shut. She walked directly from Robert's office to her own and...

Nothing.

The image in her mind's eye contained nothing that had surfaced from her subconscious. Not the slightest motion, or the faintest sound of breathing. No almost-imperceptible scent of after-shave in the air, no trace of a shouldn't-be-there shadow on the back stairs.

Yet somebody *must* have been close by. Waiting for an opportune moment.

A chill ran through her. Someone had been watching her. Spying on her.

That was like a device from a bad horror flick, designed to heighten the tension before the murder.

But thoughts along those lines were *not* helpful, so she ordered her mind to move forward—which brought her to the sense of being followed while she was walking home.

Had her intuition been right about that? Even though she hadn't seen anyone?

There was no way of knowing. But there'd been someone else in the building when her meeting with Robert had ended, no doubt about that.

She hadn't seen a soul, though. Not until she'd run into Noah on her way out.

Noah. Again.

First the note accusing him of arson. Then his still being around after this second one appeared.

No. Wait. Those two details didn't add up at all. Noah wouldn't have written a note accusing himself. Not unless he was insane, and she very much doubted he was.

She stared at the new one again, trying not to let its threat unnerve her any more than it already had.

Clearly, someone *other* than Noah had been in the building. Maybe several people. And one was all it took.

But who?

At this stage of the game she had no way of knowing. She hadn't even met all the players yet.

For a fleeting moment she thought about asking Noah if he'd seen anyone around after five. If she did that, though, he'd want to know why she was curious. And she could hardly tell him.

For that matter, this new note ruled out asking for her father's input. There'd be no point in telling him about the first note but not the second. And if she told him what *it* said…

Lord, when she got to the "dead sorry" part he'd have a fit. Then he'd insist she officially report it as a death threat. Which she couldn't do.

If she did, the police would be at Four Corners talking to people. And she definitely didn't want that.

Private investigators did *not* go running to the cops for help at the first hint of trouble. Not unless they wanted their reputations in tatters.

She glanced at the second message once more. *So don't come back. Ever.*

P.I.s also didn't quit on a client after day one. At least not because they'd gotten a couple of disconcerting anonymous notes.

But maybe she could confide in Robert. See if he had any ideas about who could have written them.

That was a possibility. However, she had a strong suspicion it wasn't a wise idea.

Robert and Larry had hired her to find out who was behind things. If she asked for their help they'd figure she didn't know what she was doing.

No, not a good option. And that left her basically on her own.

THERE WERE FAR TOO MANY thoughts racing around in Dana's head for her to make much sense out of any of them. So she put forth a concerted effort to ignore them for the moment, then looked at the new note once again.

If you do I'll make you sorry. Dead sorry.

While she was trying to convince herself that was just an *empty* threat, Doc leaped onto the couch and nudged her arm, demanding affection.

"What would happen to you if it *wasn't* an empty one?" she murmured, stroking him.

Her father might have taken pity on a freezing kitten, but he wasn't really a cat person.

As Doc climbed over her leg and settled in her lap, her gaze drifted to the little antique writing desk in front of the window.

It had been a gift from her parents. For her graduation from the academy. And she knew her mother had chosen it, which made it special.

A lump formed in her throat, almost making her shake her head in frustration. Every now and then she still fell victim to one of these sneak emotional attacks, even though her mother had been gone for three years.

Blinking back tears, she shifted Doc off her lap and wandered over to the desk.

She didn't really use it much, although she sat at it when she was paying her bills. And the drawer that locked made a perfect place to keep her gun.

Gun.

Just the word drifting through her mind was enough to make her palms start sweating.

When she'd been getting her P.I. license, her father had insisted she buy a gun. *And* be licensed to carry.

So she was. But she didn't. She hadn't carried a gun since she'd left the force.

She'd gone along with buying one to make her dad happy. He'd even helped her pick it out, ensuring she chose one light enough to be easily manageable. Then she'd brought it home from the gun store and locked it away. End of story.

Only…now…

Maybe…just in case that *wasn't* an empty threat.

Her heart pounding, she reached behind the curtain to where she kept the key hidden. Then she forced herself to open the drawer and remove the gun.

A SIG Sauer P226, 9 mm.

Solid and smooth in her hand.

As smooth as Doc's fur.

But hard, not soft.

Cold, not warm.

Deadly.

Just holding it for this brief moment almost made her tremble. How would she feel if it was in her brief-case? Within reach all day long?

No, that wouldn't be good. It would make her far too anxious.

She turned to lock the SIG away again—then froze when someone knocked on her door.

Now she didn't know whether to put her gun back in the desk or keep it with her until she saw who was there. And the mere fact she was considering the latter told her exactly how spooked she was.

Of course, she wasn't expecting anyone and her neighbors rarely came knocking. Rarely wasn't never, though.

Deciding that if it wasn't a neighbor she might be glad of a gun to flash, she headed across the room with the SIG in her hand. Then she looked through the peephole and felt relief flowing through her.

Her father was standing outside, still in uniform. He didn't drop by often, but it was frequently enough that most of the other tenants recognized him and would let him in.

Actually, she suspected he sometimes waited for one of them to arrive home—which then gave him the opportunity to remind her that, whether they knew who he was or not, the only safe rule was that *nobody* who didn't live here got in without being buzzed.

Wishing he didn't worry about her as much as he did, she stashed her gun in the hall closet. She was just reaching to slide the bolts when she remembered those two notes were sitting on the couch.

As he knocked a second time, she raced over and stuffed them inside her briefcase. Then she hurried back to the door.

"Surprised?" Jack Morancy said when she eventually opened up.

"Definitely."

She'd only been to the house yesterday. And as close as they were, they seldom saw each other more than once a week.

"What are you doing here?" she asked, stepping aside to let him pass.

"Oh, I thought instead of going home after my shift I'd see if my favorite daughter's free for dinner."

There was something important on his mind. She could tell. Something he didn't want to leave till next Sunday.

"Are you?" he said. "Free?"

"Sure."

"Good. Because that great meal you made last night got me thinking I don't take you out nearly often enough. Pretty soon, you'll be so far ahead I'll never catch up."

"Dad, I'm not keeping count, you know."

He shrugged. "Where would you like to go?"

"Mmm, how about Luigi's?"

"Is that the little place on Eighth?"

"Right."

"Nowhere fancier?"

"No, fancier would mean a later night and that's the last thing I need."

"Oh? Rough day with your new clients?"

"It was busy," she told him, not letting her gaze even flicker to her briefcase.

"How about feeding Doc while I change?" she added. "Then we can get going."

"Sure."

"I promised him Fish Delight. It's the can with the orange label."

Her father gave her a look that said people who catered to their cats were marginally unhinged, then started for her tiny kitchen while she headed to the bedroom.

As she dug through her closet, searching for the pair of cool beige cotton pants she knew were there someplace, she could hear the can opener start to whir—immediately followed by the sound of Doc charging in the direction of dinner.

"The whole can?" her father called a moment later.

"Unless you want him to rip you apart."

Finally finding the pants, she changed into them and a silky T-shirt, then slid her feet into her favorite sandals.

When she headed back out of the bedroom, her father was sitting on the couch, leafing through her latest copy of *People*.

She glanced uneasily at her briefcase as he rose, then told herself he'd never in a gazillion years stoop to poking through it.

"Darling, is anything wrong?" he said as she looked at him again.

"No. Why?"

"Oh, you seem tense, that's all."

She shook her head, trying to think of something to say that would change the subject and settling for "You must have roasted all day in that uniform."

"Over thirty years on the force, I'm used to it. Ready to go?"

"Uh-huh. Just let me check that Doc has water."

"Already done," he said, steering her toward the door.

"Great. Did you clean out his litter, too?" she teased.

"Sure. And I brushed his teeth for him.

"So, tell me about your busy day," he added as they left the apartment. "Any idea whodunit yet?"

"No. I spent a lot of time talking to the warehouse manager, though, and…"

As they headed down the stairs, she filled him in on her sense that Stu Refkin had lied about his "plans."

"That's something I'd follow up on, honey," her father said after she'd finished.

"I'm going to. I'm sure he's keeping something secret. But my gut feeling is that it doesn't have anything to do with the container fiasco."

Jack Morancy was silent for a bit. Then, when they were about halfway along the block to Eighth, he said, "How are the partners treating you? Have they got you on a tight rein or are they just letting you do your thing?"

"Well, I barely saw Larry today—only to say hello to him once as I went by his office. But I spent a little time with Robert this morning, and more this afternoon. He wants to meet with me every day, get a progress report."

"He still seem nice?"

"Uh-huh. Very."

"How about the nephew? What did you say his name was?"

She looked at her father out of the corner of her eye. She'd mentioned Noah's name enough times yesterday that he certainly wouldn't have forgotten it. So why was he pretending he had?

"Noah," she told him.

"Oh, yeah. He nice, too?" he asked, ever so casually.

Ah. Now she got it.

"He seems okay," she said.

Her father never uttered a word about her love life—or the lack of one, as was more commonly the case. That had always been her mother's department.

But she knew he wished she'd find someone. That

he'd feel better if she were married, not on her own in the city. And he'd love a grandchild or two.

So she must have said something yesterday to make him think she found Noah attractive.

They walked a little farther in silence, while another of those images of Noah tiptoed around in her mind. It was even sharper and more lifelike than the ones that had kept distracting her over the weekend.

"You remember Ken Kestler?" her father said at last. "Was my partner for a while? About ten years ago?"

"Uh-huh."

"I ran into him today."

"Oh?"

"He was telling me his son got divorced last year."

"Oh?" she said again.

"He's about your age, maybe a little older. Name's Mark, and I recall him as being a real nice kid. Teaches high school now. Anyway, Ken and I started wondering…"

No. This could *not* be going where it seemed to be. "You started wondering what?"

"Uh…you know. Maybe some night when neither of you is busy…"

"Dad!"

He shrugged. "If you're not interested, you're not interested."

She didn't say a word. This was so completely out of character for him that—

"I told Ken you probably wouldn't be, honey," he

said. "I just figured you could think about it. And if you decided you'd like to meet the man..."

"Well...all right. I'll think about it. But I'm not desperate for a date, you know."

"Of course not. You could have any guy you wanted."

Even though that was far from true, she let it pass. Then she spent the rest of the way to Luigi's trying to figure out what in the world had prompted her father to try matchmaking.

CHAPTER SIX

NOAH HAD ALWAYS FIGURED that hitting the gym three or four times a week kept him in reasonable shape. However, after following Dana up to West Twenty-fifth on the hard, hot city sidewalks, then coming back to Four Corners, his feet knew they'd been for a walk.

Only because he was wearing dress shoes, he told himself. There'd have been no problem if he'd worn sneakers, like her.

But what did a little blister matter when the trip, otherwise, had proved to be an unqualified success?

For one thing, he'd been pleased to discover he had a knack for cloak-and-dagger stuff. The two times she'd looked back he'd seen it coming and ducked into doorways.

However, the far more important outcome was that he now knew where she lived.

The next step would be seeing if there was actually a ''Dana Mayfield'' in her building. Or an apartment without an occupant listed.

Vacant apartments simply didn't exist in this city, so if one supposedly was he'd know it was hers.

After logging onto his computer, he called up the

same NYC database he'd used this morning. When he entered her address, a list of tenants' names appeared.

He scanned them, from apartment 101 through 306. Eighteen apartments, no vacancy and not a Mayfield in sight.

But he doubted she'd just been visiting someone. He'd watched her fiddling with a key at the front door. Which almost certainly meant he'd been right. Dana Mayfield wasn't her real name.

So which one of these was?

Staring blankly at the screen, he began mulling his way through pieces of trivia he'd picked up from cop shows and detective novels.

Finally, it occurred to him that when a person chooses an alias he generally picks one with the same initials as his actual name. Or *her* actual name.

That seemed to be a rule all people who were into concealing their identities knew. He supposed it was in case they had things that were monogrammed. Or maybe because when someone was asked to initial something, the response was just so automatic that…

None of that mattered, though, so he stopped thinking about it and began looking through the list of tenants again.

And there it was—might as well have been leaping out of the computer at him. ''D. Morancy.'' The sole occupant of apartment 305.

Now he was cooking. He'd bet he had her. And her occupation was…

That took a lot more poking around. He had to try several other sites.

But when the information eventually appeared he sat back and smiled.

Dana Morancy. Private Investigator. Game, set and match to Noah Haine.

He was still congratulating himself when reality roused itself and asked what on earth he had to smile about.

The fact he'd been right, that she was a P.I., only confirmed his worst suspicion. Larry had convinced his uncle *he* could be the one stabbing them in the back.

So where the hell did he go from here?

AFTER WAKING FROM HER THIRD nightmare, Dana decided she'd had enough.

Despite the fact that it was still practically the middle of the night, she got out of bed—telling herself those notes were the problem.

She knew, though, that at most they were merely part of it. The early-morning hours of July 23 always brought nightmares.

For the past five years, during the weeks leading up to the date, she'd catch herself hoping the day would come and go without her remembering. Deep down, however, she was certain it never would.

This was the fifth anniversary of the day that had changed her life forever.

If she lived to be a hundred she'd probably still be

waking up in a cold sweat, remembering what had happened. And she'd probably still relive it several times during the day, no matter how hard she tried not to.

An anniversary reaction. That was the official term. And the department shrink she'd seen had warned her to expect she'd have one.

But at the time she'd assumed she'd only have it for a year or two. Not forever.

Telling herself the best thing to do was keep busy, she put on shorts and a T-shirt, then started in on some long-ignored housework—while Doc skulked from room to room, avoiding the vacuum and occasionally eyeing her as if she'd gone mad.

After finishing up in the kitchen, she showered and dressed for work.

She didn't want to arrive at Four Corners so early that she'd have to wait out on the street. But she knew the receptionist started at eight, which meant that if she left home around seven-thirty she should be fine.

Plus, she'd get there before most of the staff. And *that* meant, if her note writer tried to sneak into her office and leave her yet another missive, she'd be on hand to surprise him.

She mentally paused to consider that. She'd be surprising someone who'd promised to make her "dead sorry" if she even showed up today. Which wasn't an entirely appealing prospect.

It was so *un*appealing, in fact, that it got her back to wondering whether she should take her gun along.

Lord, that would be an ironic thing to do on this, of all days.

Not that she'd never actually *use* it. She knew she… But there her thoughts went, wandering down that road again.

Telling them to stop, she tried to logically consider the pros and cons of having the SIG in her briefcase.

Of course, the cons weren't *entirely* rational. As much as she hated admitting that, she knew it was true. So maybe the time had come to make a major effort to get past them.

Even if she could manage to face up to them a *little*…

After all, guns frightened people. And if yesterday was any example of what her days at Four Corners would be like, she might well find herself *wanting* the means to frighten someone. So if the gun was in her briefcase…

On the other hand, just knowing it was within reach… Merely thinking how that would make her feel was unsettling.

She vacillated for another few moments, then came to a decision and retrieved the SIG from where she'd stashed it in the closet last night.

Regardless of how uncomfortable carrying it would make her feel, it was going with her. Being uncom-fortable was better than being dead.

Oh, she didn't *really* believe her life was at serious risk. But, for today, this was the way she was going to play things.

Before she could start second-guessing herself, she said goodbye to Doc and headed out. Her briefcase, with the gun inside, seemed to weigh fifty pounds.

Half an hour later, only a couple of minutes past eight, she walked into Four Corners and exchanged pleasantries with the receptionist—hoping she sounded a lot cheerier than she felt. Then she headed for the executive floor.

She was the first to arrive there, so all was quiet.

But it had been quiet yesterday, after her meeting with Robert, and her note writer had been someplace nearby. Watching and waiting.

Was he up to the same thing this morning?

Watching and waiting to learn if she'd ignore his threat and show up?

Or had he assumed she would and left her another note?

If he had, he probably *wasn't* far away right now. And she had no trouble imagining him eagerly anticipating her reaction when she discovered it.

Licking her suddenly dry lips, she forced her feet to keep moving in the direction of her office.

When she reached the door she hesitated, seriously not wanting to discover a third note on her desk. Then she unzipped her briefcase, just on the off chance a problem materialized.

Finally, taking a deep breath, she opened the door—and almost went into cardiac arrest.

"What are you doing here?" she demanded. "You scared me half to death!"

"Sorry," Noah told her.

Casually, he swung his long legs off the surface of her desk and pushed back in her chair. "I just didn't want to miss you."

"Miss me," she repeated, her heart rate slowing from triple to only double time. "You're introducing me to the rest of the staff this morning. How could you possibly miss me?"

He shrugged. "I wanted a chance to talk to you before we got going."

With that, he rose and started toward her, putting her so much in mind of a predatory animal that she barely managed to hold her ground.

Maybe he wasn't her note writer—at least she was almost certain he wasn't—but why had he ambushed her like this? And what did he want to talk about that was so important?

When he came to a halt a foot in front of her, she stopped breathing. Then she started again when he merely reached around her and shoved the door shut.

"Why don't you sit down," he said, lowering himself into one of the visitors' chairs and gesturing that the desk chair was all hers.

Rather than choosing it, she sat on the little bench in the corner and began undoing her sneakers.

With any luck, that wasn't a mistake. With any luck, she wouldn't suddenly find herself forced to make a run for it.

Kicking off her sneakers, she reached into her briefcase for her black pumps, her gaze resting a moment on the SIG lying between them and her cell phone.

"So," she said, looking at Noah again as she slipped on the shoes. "What's up?"

"My question exactly…Private Investigator Morancy."

Dammit, she silently muttered. She'd realized the man was intelligent, so she should have seen this coming. But although she'd never deluded herself into thinking her cover would meet FBI standards, nobody had penetrated it before.

"How did you find out?" she said, doing her best to sound unperturbed that he had.

"I followed you yesterday. Learned where you lived. From there it was easy."

He'd followed her. Then at least her intuition didn't need an overhaul—although that wasn't much consolation.

"You want to tell me what you're *actually* doing here?" he said.

She shrugged. Since he knew who she was, he'd already figured out the answer to his question. Which meant there was no sense in lying.

She could only hope he *wasn't* involved with the sabotage. Because if he was she'd blown the job.

"Your uncle and Larry hired me to learn who's behind the problems," she said.

"And?"

"And what?"

"And nothing. That's all there is to it."

"Oh? They don't suspect anyone in particular?"

"They told me," she said, a tad uncertainly, "that all three of you have been trying to figure out who it is. So you know as much as I do about their suspicions."

"Really."

"Yes. Really."

"Come on, Dana. Why don't you just admit the truth."

"*What* truth?"

He gazed at her for a long moment, then said, "That they suspect *me*."

"What?"

"You heard me."

"Well…yes. But what in the world gave you that idea?"

"Are you trying to tell me I'm wrong?" he said, looking extremely skeptical.

"Noah, if they do they didn't say anything to me about it. And since we discussed everyone they think it could *conceivably* be and your name didn't come up… Why would you think they suspect you?"

A little voice inside her head reminded her that she'd spent half of yesterday wrestling with *her* suspicions about him. But surely, if Larry and Robert had any, they *would* have said something.

"If they don't," Noah said slowly, "why didn't they tell me who you really are? What you're really doing here? What made them try to keep me in the dark?"

"Oh, Lord," she murmured.

"Exactly," he said, sounding like a brilliant trial lawyer nailing his case down tight.

"It was my idea," she admitted.

"What was?"

"Keeping you in the dark."

"What?" he said, the word alive with anger. "You want to elaborate on that?"

She didn't, but she said, "When Robert first came to talk to me, I asked exactly who knew they were thinking about hiring a P.I. And he said nobody. Just him and Larry. But that, naturally, they'd tell you. Only, I suggested they shouldn't."

"Because…?"

"I was thinking in terms of the fewer people knowing the better."

"I see." Noah rose from his chair, strode over to the window and stood staring out, his body language saying he definitely wasn't happy.

"That was before I'd even met you," she said to the back of his neck. "And…in hindsight, I guess maybe it wasn't the smartest suggestion I ever made."

"No, I'd say it wasn't," he muttered, not bothering to look at her.

She waited, doubting he was any more unhappy than she was, until he eventually faced her again.

"Let me get this straight," he said. "You suggested they shouldn't clue me in and Robert just said, 'Okay, fine.' Is that how it went?"

"Not precisely."

"Then how *did* it go? Precisely."

"Well...to be perfectly honest, I knew he didn't like the idea. But I...kind of pushed it. Just a little."

"I see," he said again. "Well, let's move on to the present. How do I know that everything you're saying now isn't just a pile of garbage? Know they *didn't* hire you because they suspect me? That you *aren't* here specifically to check me out?"

"Noah...do you really believe your own uncle—"

"No, I don't," he interrupted. "At least, he wouldn't on his own. But if Larry figures it could be me..."

She slowly shook her head. "I wasn't hired specifically to check you out. And neither one of them said a word about suspecting you. That's the truth."

"Just like it was the truth you're Dana Mayfield? An OD consultant?"

When she had no response to that, he turned to the window once more.

Too antsy to sit any longer, she stood and set her briefcase on the desk. Then she simply stared at the stiff set of his broad shoulders and let the silence grow.

Finally, she couldn't stop herself from saying, "Are you going to tell them you know who I am?"

This time he wheeled around and glared at her. "Is there a reason I shouldn't?"

She shrugged, going for nonchalant. "Only that it

would make me look bad. I mean, you pegged me for a phony *and* learned who I really am in no time flat.''

''Yeah, I guess that wouldn't do much for their confidence in you.''

''No, not much.''

''They might even fire you.''

''Could be,'' she said, doubting she'd quite succeeded at nonchalant that time.

In her business, word traveled. If they showed her the door because they decided she was incompetent it would get back to whoever had recommended her. And he'd never do it again.

After another lengthy silence, Noah said, ''Okay, here's where I'm at. I'm willing to make a deal. I'll pretend I don't have a clue you aren't Dana Mayfield. But only if I get something in return.''

''Only if you get *what* in return?'' she said uneasily.

NOAH LEANED CASUALLY against the wall and kept Dana hanging. It wasn't much in the way of retribution for everything he'd been going through since she'd entered his life, but he'd take what he could get.

''The deal is we team up,'' he finally told her.

She sat down behind the desk, then leveled her sky-blue gaze at him.

It made his heart bump against his ribs—which annoyed the devil out of him.

Why couldn't his uncle and Larry have hired a P.I.

who looked like Columbo rather than Demi Moore? And since they hadn't, why couldn't *he* simply ignore the interest he felt in the one they *had* hired?

He was telling himself he'd just have to keep working on that when she said, "Let's discuss what you mean by teaming up."

Staying close, he thought. *So I'll know your every move.* From somewhere—*The Sopranos,* most likely—he remembered a maxim about keeping your friends close and your enemies closer.

He didn't share that with Dana, though. He merely said, "I mean we'd both be further ahead if we pooled our resources. Because you aren't the only one trying to get to the bottom of things. I've been doing some sleuthing of my own."

"Oh? You're talking more than just discussing the problems with Robert and Larry."

He nodded.

"But they don't know what you've been up to."

"No."

"And it's involved…?"

"Keeping my eyes open. Doing some digging. Working on a couple of hypotheses I haven't shared with them."

"About who the saboteur could be?"

As he nodded once more, only the briefest flicker of interest passed across Dana's face. He'd have missed it if he hadn't been paying attention.

And when she said "Oh?" again, her tone was

dubious—as if she assumed whatever he'd been doing would be of little value.

He was in the process of giving her credit for being a good actress when she added, "And you think our man could be...?"

"Uh-uh." He shook his head. "Not unless we come to an agreement."

"Ah. But if we don't? You're serious about telling Robert and Larry you know who I really am?"

"Dead serious," he said.

She suddenly looked so upset that he almost admitted he really wasn't sure whether he'd say anything to them or not. After all, if they didn't realize he was on to her, it might be to his advantage.

He kept quiet, though, thinking that as long as she believed he'd tell them, how could she not agree to his proposal?

She'd already admitted that his pegging her for a phony, not to mention learning her true identity as fast as he had, wouldn't do much for their confidence in her.

However, since she didn't seem anywhere near crazy about his idea, he said, "Obviously, I'm an amateur when it comes to the detective business. On the other hand, I know all the employees here. And most of what goes on.

"So working together, we'd have a better shot at succeeding than if we're working separately."

He stopped there, trying to decide just how much he was prepared to confide in her at this point.

Only minutes ago, he'd been positive that he was being viewed as a possible suspect—if not the prime one. And if that really did explain why Robert and Larry hadn't told him they were hiring a P.I., if Dana was here to watch his every move, then he could forget about making any more progress.

She'd be constantly in his way, exactly what he'd been afraid of from the beginning.

Now, though, he was no longer as sure he had things figured right. If they actually hadn't confided in him only because she'd asked them not to...

The problem was he didn't know whether or not he could believe her as far as he could spit. So he wasn't about to trust her an inch until he knew, for sure, what her true agenda was.

But if she *was* being straight with him, then they *would* be better off working together.

When he focused on her again she looked lost in thought.

Wishing he could read minds, he wandered across the office and lowered himself into one of the visitors' chairs.

CHAPTER SEVEN

DANA FURTIVELY WATCHED Noah sit down, feeling as if she were between the proverbial rock and hard place.

If he made good on his threat, Robert and Larry were going to think she was an incompetent idiot. Yet if she went along with this deal of his and he *was* the one behind the plot...

Dead serious.

The words reverberated quietly in her mind, sending a slight chill through her. It was nothing, however, compared with what her reaction had been in real time.

She'd asked if he was serious about telling them he knew she was a P.I. And when he'd said "*Dead serious,*" her blood had almost frozen—because the words *dead sorry,* from the second note, had begun flashing before her eyes.

She'd told herself that his using the word *dead* was probably just a coincidence, had reminded herself that it would make no sense for him to have written the first note, accusing himself of the arson.

But if she was missing something, if he *was* the one...

Well, if he was, then she was already straight out of luck. Now that he knew who she was, how far would she get?

Not very.

He'd be so careful while she was at Four Corners that he wouldn't even breathe in the wrong direction. And he'd be throwing every red herring he could dredge up at her.

Of course, she *had* given this issue an awful lot of thought yesterday. And she *had* concluded he *wasn't* the one.

No, that wasn't quite accurate. She'd concluded the odds on it were extremely low. And extremely low wasn't the same as zero. Which meant that, unlikely as it seemed…

But her thoughts were beginning to spin like wheels on ice. And regardless of whether he was guilty or innocent, she couldn't come up with any option other than going along with his proposition.

She'd have to be wary of everything he told her, though, and not be too quick about accepting any theories he advanced. And if it turned out they were working at cross-purposes, she'd simply have to hope he'd make mistake and she'd catch it.

"Let me ask you something," she said at last.

"Ask away."

"What made you start playing detective? Without telling Robert and Larry about it?"

When he gave her a slow shrug and didn't answer

immediately, she knew he wasn't going to deliver the whole truth and nothing but.

"My uncle's spent the past thirty years building this business," he finally said.

"Your uncle and Larry."

He nodded. "My uncle and Larry. It's been their life's work, so I don't want to see it go under—which I think could happen."

"Really?"

"Really. I'm the numbers man. I've watched things progressing from bad to worse. And I've spent a lot of time trying to convince them that the situation's more serious than they want to believe."

Rapidly, she thought back to a couple of things Robert had said. About how the financial side of the business had been a mess until they'd hired Noah. About how, these days, they were only too happy to leave it to him.

So he *would* be the one to see—

"I'm sure they'd convinced themselves I was just being an alarmist," he continued. "And they were confident they'd eventually figure out who was behind the sabotage. Then everything would return to normal."

"You're using the past tense," she pointed out.

He nodded again. "I'd say the fact they hired you means they're not as sure of things as they were."

When he paused, she felt certain she knew what he was thinking. That his reasoning only held true *as-*

suming she hadn't lied to him. Assuming they hadn't hired her because they suspected him.

"I have the feeling that's *exactly* what happened," she said. "They finally realized the problem was as bad as you were telling them."

"Yeah…well…in any event, until they brought you in they weren't doing much more than talking. So I decided I'd better try to get to the bottom of things myself. I don't want my uncle having an impoverished old age."

"I see," she murmured. But she hadn't forgotten that slow shrug, so she had to assume there were omissions in what he was telling her. Or half truths. Or downright lies.

"All it would take to spell disaster," he continued, "is another couple of incidents."

"Then you figure the theory that someone's out to ruin the company is the right one? That it isn't a stock manipulation scam?"

"No, I think the plot *must* be to drive down the share value. But… Did Robert tell you that we only have a couple of major competitors?"

"Yes."

"Well, collectibles isn't a shrinking market. There's room for all the players. So the manipulation theory's the only one that really makes sense.

"But we're looking at a fine line between someone driving down the share value far enough to make a killing and driving Four Corners into bankruptcy."

"That's a real possibility? You aren't exaggerating?"

"Unfortunately, no. And we're getting close to its being more of a likelihood than a possibility."

When he left it there, all she could think was that everything he'd said seemed to hang together. No holes, no conflicting statements. And since neither Robert nor Larry had mentioned a word about suspecting him...

Besides, she only had to look at him to start her instincts telling her he simply couldn't be a baddie. And her instincts were normally reliable.

In this instance, though, she was wondering if her hormones might be confusing them. Which could mean...

But her thoughts were running in circles again.

Later, she'd take as long as she needed to work her way through this one more time. At the moment, she had to give Noah an answer.

To buy herself a few more seconds, she opened the desk drawer and put her briefcase into it.

Then she turned the key in the lock and made herself accept the fact she'd have to agree to Noah's deal. She had no choice—a position she *never* liked finding herself in.

"So what do you think?" he said. "Do we team up or not?"

She eyed him, his smug expression irritating the hell out of her. He *knew* she had no choice, and was immensely pleased about it.

"I guess we do," she told him. "But we have to work out some ground rules."

"THAT SEEMS PRETTY straightforward," Noah said. "Rule number one, we don't hold anything back."

"I'm serious about that," Dana told him.

"Right. I know you are. Partners share."

Even though he was doing his best to seem sincere, she didn't look convinced that he was—so he figured he'd better move on quickly, before she could voice her suspicions.

"And rule number two," he said, "we don't let anyone find out there's something going on between us."

She clearly didn't like the way he'd phrased that, which almost made him grin. He was still annoyed that she'd kept her true identity a secret from him, and even though he realized that trying to get back at her for it was more than a little childish, he was enjoying it.

"Why do I have the feeling," she said, "that you think this is amusing?"

"Amusing? No way. I couldn't be more serious. If we're partners we're partners.

"In fact, we should exchange cards, right? So we have each other's phone numbers and whatever."

He took a card from his wallet and slid it across the desk to her. "There you go. Office and cell numbers."

When he eyed her expectantly, she dug out one of hers.

"Oh, good," he said, glancing at it. "A *real* one. Dana *Morancy,* private investigator.

"And as for not letting anyone know we've got something going," he added, "I have no problem with that, either. You obviously don't want Robert and Larry to think you're trying to find yourself a boyfriend on their time."

She glared at him. "That is *not* what I said. I merely said we have to be circumspect.

"You know how people are. It doesn't take much to start them speculating. And if we end up having to get together outside of office hours, we *definitely* can't say anything about it."

He shrugged. "Fair enough. You don't want anyone to figure we're involved."

"Noah…" she said, her tone threatening.

"What?"

"Just…I'm only saying we can't spend too much time together. I mean, after you've finished introducing me around, there won't be any apparent reason for us to—"

"Don't worry about it. I know exactly what you're getting at."

He left it there, then tried not to think that he'd *like* to spend "too much time" with her. Although he suspected "too much" wouldn't be possible.

The last bit of his annoyance was already fading,

and he had no trouble at all imagining how he'd enjoy spending a whole *lot* of time with her.

She had more depth than any other woman he'd ever met, and he'd only begun to scratch the surface of it. Since he'd like to do far more than that...

Of course, he couldn't lose track of the fact that she might be out to prove *he* was the saboteur.

But since he wasn't, did that really matter?

He looked at her again and caught her watching him—which made him smile.

Dana swore to herself. Noah wasn't taking her ground rules half as seriously as she'd like him to, and she truly doubted that pressing harder would get her anywhere.

Yet if he *wasn't* circumspect... Well, he'd certainly been right about her not wanting Robert and Larry to figure she was trying to find herself a boyfriend on their time. They'd view that as *so* highly unprofessional that—

Her thoughts were interrupted by someone knocking at the door.

"Yes?" she called.

It opened, revealing an extremely flustered-looking Helen Rupert.

"Oh, thank heavens I found you," she said to Noah. "The receptionist told me you were already here when she arrived, but you weren't downstairs and—"

"What's wrong?" he interrupted.

"There's been an accident in the warehouse. Larry and Robert aren't in yet, and…"

Her words trailed off as Noah bolted out of his chair and Dana pushed hers back.

"You stay here," he told her.

Ignoring that, she hurried after him.

"I said, *stay here*," he repeated as they started down the stairs.

"Uh-uh. We just made a deal, remember? We're a team."

He muttered something she couldn't make out, but it certainly didn't sound like a compliment.

Ignoring that, as well, she darted out of the building on his heels. It wasn't until he headed off down the street at a rapid pace that she realized she'd changed into her dress shoes. And since he didn't bother waiting for her, he had half a block's lead when he reached the warehouse.

By the time she arrived he was on the far side of the main space, bent down next to Tony Zicco. Stu Refkin and Paul Coulter were hovering over them.

Nearby stood three wooden crates—roughly the size of cartons that television sets come in. They were piled one on top of the other, while two more, which looked as if they'd fallen, were lying on the floor.

Even at a distance, it was clear from Tony's expression that he was in pain. And as she walked across the floor she could almost hear Noah saying, "All it would take to spell disaster is another couple of incidents."

"What happened?" she demanded, reaching the men.

Both Stu and Paul glanced at her, then at Noah, giving her a minor reality check. From their perspective, this wasn't any of her business.

As Noah rose, she warned herself to be careful about asking pointed questions. "Those crates must not have been stacked properly," Noah said. "Tony and Paul were trying to move them, but pulling the first one off brought the second one down."

"The top one was stuck," Tony explained, wincing as he spoke. "And when I gave it a tug…"

"I was helping push from the side," Paul added. "But Tony was right in the way."

"It's a good thing he moved fast," Stu said. "Otherwise, he'd have been hit square in the face."

A tiny shudder ran through Dana. "Square in the face" would have meant a broken nose at minimum. Eye damage or head trauma wouldn't have been surprising.

"Instead, his knee got it," Stu added.

She nodded. That was apparent from the blood oozing through the leg of his pants.

"Do you want me to have a look, Tony?" she asked, kneeling down. "I know first aid."

When he seemed leery, she almost blurted out that accident-scene training went with being a cop. But she caught herself in time. She didn't want to start these guys wondering how she'd gone from police officer to OD consultant.

"Yeah," Tony said at last. "Yeah, I guess you might as well take a look."

"Then I need something to cut his pants with."

Paul took a small pair of shears from his tool belt and handed them to her.

She carefully cut her way up the pant leg until she'd exposed the injury. Then she gingerly examined it.

There was a deep gash, almost to the bone, across his kneecap—where the edge of the crate had caught it. But nothing seemed to be broken.

"I think you were lucky," she said. "A few stitches, a lot of ice and some time off your feet should be all you'll need."

"I hope you're right," Tony said, his relief visible.

"They've already called an ambulance," Noah told her. "So you might as well go on back to the office. This obviously means a change in plans.

"Dana wanted to finish talking to you men this morning," he elaborated to the others. "We were just on our way over when Helen caught up with me."

He shot Dana a meaningful glance that said he'd explained her presence. The rest was up to her.

"Yes, of course," she said. "We can talk again *anytime*. Right now, Tony's knee is all that matters."

As much as she'd like to stay and have a look at those crates, see if she could tell whether or not the stack had been rigged, Noah was playing this right.

It would *definitely* raise suspicions if she began checking out the crime scene—and considering everything else that had happened, she had little doubt it *was* a crime scene.

Reluctantly, she pushed herself up from beside Tony and assured him that she was certain he'd be just fine.

"I'll stay here until the ambulance has been," Noah told her.

She nodded, then started off, getting barely halfway up the wharf before an ambulance came speeding toward her.

Resisting the temptation to turn around and follow it back to the warehouse, she continued on toward head office.

NOAH HAD GOTTEN the distinct impression that Dana knew a fair bit about a lot of things the average person didn't.

He doubted, for example, that most women had ever been in burned-out buildings—something he hadn't found a good opening to ask her about, although he assumed private investigators could easily get involved with arson cases.

At any rate, it didn't surprise him when the ambulance attendants agreed with her assessment of Tony's injury. A few stitches, an ice pack and some downtime were all he'd probably need.

However, saying he should have his knee x-rayed, just to be on the safe side, they loaded him onto a gurney for a trip to St. Vincent's.

Once they'd left, Stu told Paul he'd better get back to work.

"Until we have a temp in here," he added, "we'll be doing everything ourselves."

"Maybe after we get one, too," Paul said. "Half the temp guys we've had have been lazier than a dog in the sun."

As he turned away, Stu caught Noah's gaze and quietly said, "I gave the crates that are still standing a once-over before you got here. The bottom three aren't balanced just right."

He paused for a moment, then added, "We're never careless about how we stack things."

Noah nodded, thinking he'd prefer to handle this on his own, yet realizing there was no way. He could hardly tell Stu to take a hike, so he said, "Let's have a look at the two that came down."

They didn't have to look far to confirm what they both suspected.

There was a fresh scratch on the bottom of the crate that Tony and Paul had been trying to lift off the stack. Roughly three inches long, it ran in a straight line to the edge.

Examining the other crate, they found the point of a nail sticking out of its top. About three inches in.

Stu shot Noah an anxious glance, then rubbed his thumb across the point, saying "The top crate was caught on this. When Tony pulled harder, trying to free it…"

"Yeah, I'd say you're right."

"There's no way a crate would be *shipped* with a nail sticking out of it," Stu said. "It would have caught on something long before this.

"And look here." He gestured toward a couple of indentations in the wood. "The top's been pried off, then nailed shut again."

"Why don't we open it up," Noah suggested, wondering if they'd find something inside that shouldn't be. Or discover a space where something *had* been.

One of his own private theories, albeit a pretty off-the-wall one, was that the warehouse problems were related to a smuggling racket.

Just possibly, some of Four Corners shipments were being used to bring drugs or something into the country.

His pulse beating rapidly, he watched while Stu grabbed a pry bar and went to work.

When he got the crate open they saw that the nail wasn't sticking out of anything inside. Someone had driven its tip through the top and then bent back the rest and hammered it flat against the wood.

As for the contents, they were buried beneath an undisturbed layer of packing straw—which probably meant his smuggling theory was all wet. The only apparent reason the crate had been opened was to drive that nail into the top.

Stu looked at Noah, his expression even more anxious, and said, "Someone's out to get me."

CHAPTER EIGHT

WITH NOAH STILL AT the warehouse, Dana considered simply introducing *herself* to the rest of the head office employees. Experience, however, told her they'd be more receptive if someone with authority did it, so she headed straight up to the second floor.

When it turned out that neither Robert nor Larry had arrived yet, she asked Helen Rupert if she had time to talk.

"Sure." Helen gestured her to sit. "Noah just called, by the way. To say they've taken Tony Zicco to St. Vincent's."

"Really?"

Dana barely had time to hope she hadn't been wrong about how serious his injury was before Helen added, "I gather it's only a precautionary thing. They seem to think he'll be fine. But what do you want to talk about?"

"Well…anything and everything, I guess. I haven't forgotten that Noah said you're the one who really runs the company."

The older woman laughed. "If I did, we'd have had an efficiency expert in here long before this."

Efficiency expert. She assumed a *real* OD consultant would correct Helen's use of the old-fashioned term, but all she said was "Oh?"

"You'd better believe it. I've been saying for twenty years or more that we could improve the way we do a lot of things. But the bosses are of the if-it's-not-broken-don't-fix-it school, and they've never listened to me."

"Well, you *are* a woman," Dana said, giving her a conspiratorial smile.

She laughed again. "So is Larry's wife and they certainly listen to her.

"Maybe I'm telling tales out of school, but Robert and Larry aren't exactly sold on consultants. I wouldn't have believed *anyone* could convince them to hire one—although I should have known better than to underestimate Martha Benzer."

Helen paused, looking as if she thought she might have said the wrong thing, then added, "They *did* tell you it was her idea, didn't they?"

Dana nodded; Helen seemed relieved.

"Of course, there've been some changes since Noah arrived," she continued. "But aside from what they *had* to agree to because we were going public, even he's had trouble dragging them out of the Dark Ages."

"I see that sort of thing all the time. Most people resist change.

"But why don't you tell me about some of the things that could be improved. Oh, and please speak freely."

Helen was clearly uncertain about the wisdom of that, so Dana added, "It's okay. Really. I never attribute what I hear to specific people."

"In that case, I don't know where to start. Maybe…it's not exactly something I've thought could be improved, but…I guess the bosses told you how many problems we've been having recently?"

"Yes," Dana said, suddenly feeling sure that Robert was wrong, that not *all* the Four Corners employees figured the "incidents" amounted to nothing more than a string of bad luck.

The majority of them might, but Helen apparently had her suspicions—which was hardly surprising. She was in a perfect position to see the complete picture almost as well as "the bosses."

"It seems to me," she continued, "that all of these…"

As her words trailed off, her expression changed from open to guarded.

Glancing around, Dana saw that Larry Benzer was standing outside the office.

"Good morning." She shot him a smile.

"'Morning. I heard downstairs," he added to Helen, "that we've had more trouble at the warehouse."

Dana tried to read his expression as he spoke. Since he was *already* convinced that one of the warehouse people was involved with the sabotage, she wondered how much more convinced he'd just become.

When looking at him didn't give her an answer,

she turned her full attention back to Helen, who was telling him what had happened to Tony.

"But he's going to be fine," she concluded. "And Noah's already been over there. He just phoned to say he'll be back shortly."

"Okay, then I won't bother going. I want to see Noah as soon as he gets here, though."

"I'll let the receptionist know," Helen said, reaching for her phone.

"Thanks. And when you're finished come into my office, would you? There's something I need you to do.

"I'm not interrupting anything important, am I?" he asked Dana.

"No. Helen was telling me about her job, but we can finish up later."

"Fine."

Larry turned and started away, leaving her with a vague sense that he hadn't been pleased to find her talking with Helen.

But that couldn't be right.

He'd been aware, from square one, that she'd be interviewing everyone on staff. And he had to want her to determine who was behind their problems as badly as Robert did.

She was halfway to her own office before it occurred to her that she hadn't remembered to tell Helen about her broken lock.

She *had* to make a point of doing that. And soon. The last thing she wanted was another surprise.

Feeling more than a touch apprehensive, she cautiously opened her door—then breathed a sigh of relief when she saw that everything looked exactly as it had earlier.

WITH HER OFFICE PRETTY WELL cut off from the main area of the second floor, Dana couldn't see much when she was at her desk.

She had no difficulty hearing, though, so she'd left her door standing ajar—on the theory that Noah might not be intending to come and see her as soon as he was finished in Larry's office.

By rights, he should. She still needed him to introduce her around.

Plus, he'd know that she'd want him to fill her in on what had happened after she'd left the warehouse. On whether or not he'd learned anything more about Tony's so-called accident.

Yet if she simply left it up to him, what he *should* do and *would* do might be two entirely different things. After all, the man had to resent her.

He'd started his sleuthing well before she'd appeared on the scene, so from his point of view she was horning in on *his* investigation. Oh, he might not be consciously admitting he felt that way, but deep down in his subconscious…

Well, resenting her would only be human nature, despite her being a professional and him an amateur. And even if she set *that* aside, she'd still have no illusions about how solid their newly forged partnership was.

How could it be anything but shaky when it was based on the man finding her out? Then deciding that teaming up with her would be to his advantage and coercing her into agreeing to the idea?

If there'd been any good way around that she'd have jumped on it. Because she did *not* like the idea of sharing what she learned with him.

She worked alone by choice. And if she wanted any help, or someone to bounce ideas around with, there was her father. Besides which, she had her doubts about the kind of *help* she could expect from Noah.

Regardless of his assurances, she knew darned well that he wouldn't be half as eager to tell her anything *he* found out as to hear what *she* did.

But she was stuck with him. For the moment, at least. So instead of sitting worrying about it she should be doing something productive.

To that end, she unlocked her desk and got out the notes she'd made yesterday. Maybe, if she reviewed them, something new would strike her.

When she started reading, though, the words barely made sense—because her mind had gone back to the subject of Noah Haine resenting her.

She wished she didn't care whether he did or not. Yet wishing didn't make it so.

As hard as she was trying to ignore the pull she felt toward him, he was like some magic magnet that kept growing stronger all the time. Which was simply one more reason that she was far from happy about being forced into partnership with him.

She tucked her hair behind her ears and took a fresh stab at focusing her attention firmly on the notes. But three seconds later she began thinking about yet another reason Noah had to be ticked off at her.

The fact Robert and Larry hadn't told him she was a P.I. had really annoyed him. So admitting that not letting him in on the secret had been *her* idea was a black mark against her. And, to his mind, there were undoubtedly enough of those marks to add up to...

Yesterday, she'd been sure he was every bit as attracted to her as she was to him. At this point, she wasn't nearly as convinced. Although she still had the sense that...

But if he'd decided he didn't like her...

Well, she *really* didn't want a partner who was feeling lust without like.

After staring blankly at the pages in front of her for another minute, she decided she might as well forget about trying to read them. Instead, she'd figure out just how much she was prepared to tell Noah.

He intended to share selectively. She didn't have the slightest doubt about it.

Given that, she wouldn't feel guilty doing exactly the same thing.

Not that she *had* a lot to share. Thus far, there was really nothing except those two damned anonymous notes. So should she show them to him?

She considered the question.

If there was any downside, she couldn't think of it. And it would be far easier for him to get print samples to check them against. Which added up to a yes.

She opened her desk drawer again, this time reaching into her briefcase. When her fingers brushed against her SIG, a prickly feeling ran up her arm.

It had been so long since she'd carried a gun that she'd forgotten she'd brought it with her, and she didn't like being reminded.

Gingerly, she dug down past it, retrieved the two notes and unfolded them. Once they were lying on her desk she sat staring at them, thinking there had to be something she was missing.

And then it struck her.

"Oh, Lord," she whispered, focusing on her own notes again.

Her heart hammering, she took the top page and set it down, overlapping the second note, the longer of the two.

After comparing them carefully against her own notes, she was convinced that they'd all come from the same printer. Which meant that whoever had written the notes had used *her* printer.

So much for Noah getting print samples. The printer was sitting right here on her desk.

Somebody had come boldly into her office and...

But who?

Doing her best to ignore the frozen sensation in the pit of her stomach, she thought hard.

The first note had been here when she'd gotten back from the warehouse yesterday. Whoever had left it would have had almost the entire morning to slip in and print it.

The second one, however, was a different story.

You had your chance, it read. *You had today. But you didn't get anywhere, did you.*

That had to have been written toward the end of yesterday afternoon. So logic said someone came in here and printed it while she was in Robert's office.

Did that help her any, though? They'd talked for a good hour. Enough time for virtually anyone to sneak up the back stairs, completely unseen, and—

"Hello."

The greeting made her jump.

"Oh, sorry, I didn't mean to startle you," the woman added as Dana's gaze flashed to the doorway.

An attractive, fiftyish, streaked blonde was looking in at her. She smiled warmly, then said, "I'm Martha Benzer. Larry's wife."

"Yes, I recognized your name."

While her heartbeat slowed back to normal, Dana managed a smile of her own. "He's mentioned you," she added, casually turning the two anonymous notes over so they were blank-side up.

Martha nodded, as if she took for granted that Larry routinely talked about her.

"I drove over with him this morning," she explained, coming into the office and sitting down. "We're having lunch with one of our oldest clients—

one I'm quite close to. You know I used to work with Larry and Robert?''

"Yes."

"Well, in any event, I could have just met Larry and the client at the restaurant, but I thought I'd visit with some of the people downstairs. And by the time I got up here, Noah was in Larry's office and they had the door closed. So Helen suggested I introduce myself.''

"I'm glad she did."

Martha hesitated for a moment, then said, "How are you making out?"

Dana manufactured another smile, wishing she'd clarified exactly what Larry had told his wife and what he hadn't.

But since Robert had said that no one except he and Larry would know they'd hired an investigator, she said, "Well, all new projects start off slowly. Simply talking to everyone takes a while."

"I guess it does. I certainly hope you can pinpoint what's wrong, though. We never *used* to have any problems. Of course, that was when *I* was here."

Even though Martha was smiling again, Dana wasn't entirely sure the remark was meant to be humorous, so she merely said, "Do you have any idea why there are problems *now?*"

She kept her tone casual, as if she was more making conversation than anything else. But if Martha *did* have any thoughts on the subject, they'd be welcome.

"Not really," she said slowly. "Unless it has

something to do with the company losing its 'family' feeling.''

''Oh?''

Martha looked thoughtful for a moment, then added, ''I gather that can easily happen when a company goes public. And in our particular instance…

''I don't want you to take this the wrong way. I have nothing against Noah Haine. But it was after he arrived that things started to change.''

''That was why he was hired, though, wasn't it? To help make some changes?''

Martha shook her head. ''I'm not just talking about the ones he implemented, but about attitudes.

''Suddenly, people who'd reported directly to Larry and Robert—literally forever—were told to report to a newcomer. Who, in a lot of cases, was years younger than them. And some of them found it…distressing.''

''Distressing enough to stop caring about the company? To get sloppy about their work? Is that why you think things haven't been going smoothly?''

''Well…possibly. All I know is that things *did* run smoothly for an awfully long time. Now they aren't. But you're the consultant, not me.''

Dana nodded slowly, aware that she was feeling angry on Noah's behalf and knowing she shouldn't be.

The fact that she didn't like to hear him not at all subtly being blamed for the company's woes had to suggest a serious lack of objectivity on her part. Which *wasn't* a good thing.

There were a few seconds of silence while she tried to think of what to say next. Before she managed to come up with something, the man himself appeared.

"Oh, sorry," he said when he stepped into her office and saw Martha.

"It's okay," she told him. "I just popped in here while you and Larry were talking."

As Martha spoke, Dana's gaze returned to Noah—and she silently admitted that she didn't have a prayer of being totally objective about him.

These might be the completely wrong circumstances in which to be attracted to a man. And he might be the completely wrong man. Yet she couldn't deny that the mere sight of him sent a little tingle through her.

And she wasn't normally susceptible to tingles.

"Well, it was nice meeting you," Martha said, drawing Dana's attention back to her.

"Nice meeting you, too," she replied as the woman rose. "I'm glad you stopped by."

Once she was gone, Noah gestured toward the door, wordlessly asking if it was okay to close it.

At Dana's nod, he pushed it shut.

"Helen told me they took Tony to the hospital," she said as he sat down in the chair Martha had vacated.

"Yeah, but he'll probably be fine. The ambulance guys said more or less what you did."

"And how about the accident?"

"It wasn't one. Someone rigged those crates."

"I figured as much."

Noah raked his fingers through his hair, saying, "If Tony had been hurt more seriously, if we had to involve the insurance company...

"We made claims both for the fire and those missing containers. Any more and they might cancel our coverage."

"Could you operate without insurance?"

"No. Even if we wanted to risk it, we couldn't. Public companies are required to have adequate insurance."

"Maybe *that's* part of the plot, then. To make you lose your coverage."

"Yeah, I wouldn't be surprised."

After a few seconds of silence, Dana said, "Let's get back to those crates. Do you have any idea who might have rigged them?"

"Well, there was no sign of forced entry. By this point I know what to look for. So the most obvious people are the ones with warehouse keys. Which means Stu Refkin and Paul Coulter."

"You're assuming Tony wouldn't have done it, then knowingly injured himself."

Noah gave her a weary smile. "Yeah. You think that's a safe assumption?"

When she didn't answer immediately, he said, "You *don't* think so, do you."

"Not *entirely* safe," she admitted slowly. "If he *is*

somehow mixed up in all this, what better way to throw suspicion off himself?''

"A pretty painful way."

"True. But remember what Stu said? That it was a good thing Tony moved fast?

"Well, maybe he did because he knew the crate was going to come down. Or..." She shrugged. "I don't know. Maybe the fact that he's done time is just making me overly suspicious of him—even though it *was* years ago."

"So where are you at?" Noah asked when she paused.

"Well, I still have to talk to both Tony and Paul individually. But right now I guess I can't really see *any* of those men...

"After all, we're up to *three* incidents involving the warehouse now, and since they aren't morons..."

"Yeah, you're right. That does make them awfully unlikely suspects."

"And I keep coming back to the lie detector tests. If we believe the results, then none of them can be our guy.

"Whoever set the fire probably just managed to get hold of a key somewhere along the line. And there's no reason he couldn't have used it again last night."

"Yes, there is," Noah said. "We changed the warehouse locks after the arson."

Robert hadn't mentioned that, yet it was such an obvious thing to do it should have occurred to her to ask.

"Okay, then that's out," she said, thinking aloud. "But your master keys work on the new locks?"

"Uh-huh. Which suggests…?"

"That maybe it wasn't a warehouse key the saboteur got hold of. Maybe he has a copy of the master."

She waited while Noah considered that.

"You think it's likely?" he said at last.

"Well, *borrowing* a key long enough to make a copy is hardly unheard of."

"In other words, we could be talking about virtually anyone."

"Not quite. Just anyone who might ever have had access to one of the masters."

Noah eyed her, then said, "I'll be back in a minute."

THE MINUTE PROVED TO BE more like ten, but when Noah strode into Dana's office again he looked marginally less concerned.

"Okay," he said, sitting down across the desk from her once more. "Regardless of what key this guy has it isn't going to help him again.

"We're getting the locks on all the exterior doors changed today. And Robert, Larry and I will have brand-new masters—which none of us will let out of our sight."

"Good," Dana said. "And while the locksmith's here, could he fix the lock on my door?"

"It's not working?"

"No."

"Then sure. Why don't you call Helen right now. Ask her to look after it. She's extension twenty-six."

As soon as Dana had finished doing that, Noah said, "Okay, where were we?"

"We were talking about Stu and Paul."

"Right. And I was just going to tell you that Stu said he figures someone's trying to get him fired. He's convinced *that's* the point of all this stuff involving the warehouse."

"What do *you* think?"

"I don't know. I suppose it's a possibility. I mean, as you said, we've had *three* problems there now."

"So it isn't hard to see why Stu would be worried. But if we stick with the theory that it's the *company* someone's out to cause grief..."

"Yeah, that makes a lot more sense. Stu's a good guy, which makes the idea of someone going to such extremes to get *him*..."

She nodded. "And even if our saboteur *has* been using a master key, maybe he just kept hitting the warehouse so suspicion would fall on the people there. Even though it *does* seem like way too obvious a ploy."

"Do you ever actually get any answers in this business?" Noah said. "Or is it only questions?"

That made her smile. "It sometimes feels that way," she admitted. "But all this talk about keys has started me thinking..."

"What?"

She hesitated. However, since she'd already decided it made sense to show Noah the notes she might as well continue.

"The door to the alley?" she said. "At the bottom of the back stairs?"

"Uh-huh?"

"Does it get used much?"

"Larry and Robert and I park behind the building, so that's the way we normally come and go. But nobody uses it aside from us."

"And it's always kept locked." Not that she really needed him to confirm that. This *was* New York.

"Of course," he said.

"And is it pretty secluded? I mean, is anyone likely to see you coming or going?"

"No. But what's your point?"

She took a deep breath, then said, "Noah, someone left me two anonymous notes yesterday. One was sitting on my desk when I came back from the warehouse. The other was stuck into my briefcase.

"I didn't find it until I got home, but I know it was put there just before I left. Until then, the case was locked in my desk.

"At any rate, I've been assuming whoever wrote the notes has to work here. That he just slipped up from the main floor with them.

"Now, though, I'm thinking that isn't necessarily the case. Someone with a master could have used the alley door and come up the back stairs without being seen."

Noah slowly shook his head. "So we're at virtually

anyone again. Hell, we're at virtually anyone in the entire city now. But let's see the notes.''

As he leaned forward, she reluctantly turned them over and picked up the one that accused him of being the arsonist.

''This was the first,'' she said, handing it to him. ''Try not to let it upset you.''

CHAPTER NINE

ANGER SPREADING THROUGH HIM like radiant heat, Noah pushed himself out of the chair.

After reading the first note again he looked at Dana, saying, "Let's see the other one."

She silently slid it across the desk, then leaned back in her chair without taking her gaze from him.

He began to read.

You had your chance. You had today. But you didn't get anywhere, did you.

Not too smart. And I don't like people who aren't smart. So don't come back. Ever. If you do I'll make you sorry. Dead sorry.

By the time he'd reached the final words, he no longer gave a damn about the note saying he'd set the warehouse fire. Some lunatic trying to implicate him was inconsequential compared with a threat against Dana's life.

He looked at her once more, amazed at how shaken he felt.

He'd known the woman less than a week, hadn't as much as touched her hand. And half the time he *had* known her he'd been mad as hell at her. Yet the thought of something awful happening to her filled him with ice-cold dread.

"Have you talked to the police about this?" he said.

She shook her head.

"Then you have to do that. Maybe they can tell whose printer was used and—"

"It was this one," she interrupted, gesturing toward the computer on her desk.

"You're kidding."

"Uh-uh."

"Well, maybe there's still a chance they can get his fingerprints off the notes. Or the keyboard. There's got—"

"There weren't any prints. He wore gloves. Latex. Disposables."

"How do you know that?"

"He left a pair with each of the notes."

"Oh, terrific. Dana, this guy sounds warped. So I *really* think you should call—"

"No. That's just not a good idea."

His chest began to feel tight. Didn't she realize how serious this could be?

Making a conscious effort to speak calmly, he said, "I think it's an *excellent* idea. When someone threatens to make you *dead sorry,* ignoring it can't be the smartest move."

"Noah, I'm not ignoring it. I'm just not involving the police."

"Why not?"

"Because I don't want to. I've got my reasons and they're good ones," she added quickly. "Let's leave it at that."

Remaining calm was getting tougher by the second, but he did his best.

"Okay, you've got your reasons," he said, sitting down across from her once more. "Can we consider a couple of things, though?

"You're in an out-of-the-way office." He hurried on before she could say a word. "You're basically cut off from everyone else. And some creep has been sneaking up the back stairs and in here at will."

"He won't be able to get in once my lock is fixed."

"Well, he doesn't necessarily have to. He could... What I'm getting at is, don't you figure someone should be looking into the situation?"

"*I'm* looking into it. Who would have written those notes except the saboteur? And I'm going to learn who he is. That's why I'm here."

"Uh-huh? And what if he tries to make good on his threat *before* you learn who he is?"

Her reply was so quiet he missed it.

"Pardon?"

"I said I have a gun."

That surprised him—but only momentarily. After all, she *was* a P.I.

"Where is it?" he demanded.

"In my briefcase."

"How well can you shoot?"

She eyed him, her face pale and her expression so anxious it made him want to walk around the desk and gather her up in his arms. But instinct warned him to hold off on anything like that.

"I can shoot just fine," she said at last. "I used to be a cop. NYPD. I had to pass an annual target test."

"You used to be a cop," he repeated. Another surprise.

Logic might say that a lot of investigators would be ex-cops, yet he'd never have taken her for one. She was too delicate. Too vulnerable-looking. And that anxious expression he'd just seen didn't fit the picture of a typical law enforcement type.

"How long were you on the force?" he said.

"Almost four years."

"And you quit because…?"

The moment he asked the question he could see it was one she didn't want to answer. So she didn't.

She merely shrugged and said, "We've lost focus. Let's get back to our saboteur.

"Before we went racing off to the warehouse, I had the impression you have your suspicions about who he might be. So since we're partners…"

He hesitated. Earlier, he hadn't been entirely sure how much he was willing to share with her. But that threatening note changed the picture drastically.

Unless whoever wrote it was bluffing, her life was at risk. Which meant that wasting time playing games wouldn't be wise.

However, there were other considerations. He began to rapidly think his way through them, even though he was almost positive there was only one thing to do.

DANA SAT WATCHING NOAH, waiting for him to decide which way to jump.

As the saying went, push had come to shove. Either he really wanted to be her partner or he didn't.

If she had to predict, she'd say he did. And she'd gotten to know him well enough that she thought she could read him accurately.

She only wished it had taken her less time to reach this stage, because it would have saved a lot of agonizing over whether or not he was the one behind the company's problems.

But at least she felt confident about him now. Her last lingering doubts had evaporated while he'd been studying those notes.

His anger at being accused of setting the fire had been genuine. And his concern when he'd read the threatening one... Well, it had been just as genuine.

She'd been wrong earlier, thinking he might have decided he didn't like her. He did. And he was afraid for her, which made her want to hug herself.

Or hug him. That might be more to the point.

She'd had her fill of men who kept their emotions so hidden away that she could never tell what they honestly felt. Which meant that finding one who didn't... And one who was positively gorgeous, to boot...

Letting her gaze rest on his strong, regular features, she reflected that it was a good thing there was a desk between them. If it weren't in the way, she'd be sorely tempted to reach over and trace his jaw. And that would not be smart.

The rules hadn't all gone out the window just because she'd concluded she could definitely trust him.

She never willingly put herself in a position that would make her the topic of gossip. And in this case it was even more important than usual.

Robert had hired her to do a job, not to get involved with his nephew. That fact hadn't changed at all.

Noah reread one of the notes again, then focused on her. "This 'I know who you really are' bit," he said. "How would anyone have found out so fast?"

She gave him a wry smile. "Faster than you did, you mean?"

He didn't smile back. "Dana, this isn't funny. I still think you should be calling the police. But if you won't, then at least take things seriously."

"I am. Believe me, I am. We're talking anonymous notes, though. Left when I'm not around. Notes that say this guy's from the sneaky school. He isn't the type who'd come marching in here for a face-to-face confrontation.

"The notes are probably nothing more than an attempt to scare me off. But if he does try anything else, it won't be in my office in broad daylight."

"Then you need a bodyguard for when you're not in your office in broad daylight."

When he looked as if he might be willing to volunteer, she wanted to hug him even more.

Instead, she said, "I'm an ex-cop with a gun, remember? I'll be fine. Although, I admit I *will* be happier after we've figured out who our guy is. Or our woman is."

"You think that's a possibility?"

She shrugged. "I'm always careful about getting tunnel vision. And the most obvious person to have learned who I really am, fast, is Helen."

Noah simply eyed her for a moment, before saying, "Helen likes me. Why would she want to make you think I'm the arsonist?"

He paused for a second, then added, "You didn't, did you?"

"Well...I speculated about it a little. But only briefly."

He obviously wasn't entirely happy with that, so before he could follow up on it she said, "At any rate, I wasn't implying I think it *is* Helen. Aside from anything else, I've got no idea if she might have a motive.

"All I meant is she's in a perfect position to overhear things Robert and Larry talk about. And she could easily have slipped in here and printed off those notes.

"It wasn't *necessarily* someone using the back stairs."

"You probably don't know this," Noah said slowly. "But Helen was the very first person they hired when they were starting up. And I just can't imagine her doing anything like that.''

''I'm sure you're right,'' Dana told him. ''So who *can* you imagine doing it?''

She held her breath after the words were out, hoping he'd tell her every relevant thought he'd had since the sabotage began.

All he did, though, was glance at his watch and say, ''It's almost noon. You weren't planning to skip lunch again today, were you?''

ROXY'S DELI, down on Gansevoort, had good food at not bad prices and arguably the best dill pickles south of Midtown—plus a few little tables looking out onto the street.

Since it was close to Four Corners, Noah ate lunch there often enough that he didn't even need to look at the menu, let alone study it.

However, he sat staring at it as if it was brand-new, wanting another couple of minutes to decide whether he should be absolutely forthright with Dana.

On the one hand, he couldn't see holding back anything that might help her. Not when he had a horrible feeling she really was in danger.

The problem was, Robert and Larry had hired her. Which meant she owed her allegiance to them.

It hardly took an expert on the ethics of private investigators to figure that out. And it put him in a sticky position.

He didn't want to see Four Corners go under; he'd

been trying his hardest to prevent that. But he'd rather not lose his job in the process.

"What do you recommend?" Dana said, glancing up from her menu.

"The Reubens are great. Come with a mountain of fries."

"Oh, a diet lunch," she said, then shot him a smile.

It sent such a hot rush through him, his brain practically melted—no doubt explaining why he found himself having trouble just coming up with another suggestion.

"The special's usually reliable," he finally managed to say.

"I'll try it, then."

"Good choice. I'll go order."

"Just water to drink," she added as he pushed his chair away from the table.

He headed to the counter and told Roxy what they wanted, then started over toward Dana once more, certain he'd run out of thinking time. She'd want to get back to business.

And she didn't wait a second. As he sat down she said, "So? After lunch, am I finally going to meet the rest of the employees?"

"Unless there's another *incident*."

"Don't even say that. Just tell me who you figure I should pay special attention to."

"Well…let me ask you something before we start in on that."

"Sure."

"Robert mentioned that you'll be getting together with him every afternoon."

"Right. He wants updates on my progress."

"What about Larry?"

"I don't have the impression he's as interested. Or as optimistic about my getting anywhere. My read is that it was mostly Robert who decided they should hire a P.I. and Larry basically just went along with the idea."

Noah nodded. Then, knowing he might as well get to the point, he said, "Remember I told you neither of them has any idea I've been sleuthing?"

"Uh-huh."

"Well, it has to stay that way. Since the three of us have done a lot of talking about what's been going on, they wouldn't like it if they knew I'd gone further than that—without telling them about it, I mean."

At least, he strongly suspected, *one* of them wouldn't like it. But he wasn't quite ready to get into that with Dana.

"There isn't a problem," she was assuring him. "They don't have to know a thing about what you've been doing."

"You're positive it won't come out? If you inadvertently repeat something I tell you…"

"Noah, I was a cop for almost four years and I've been a P.I. for nearly five. I won't say the wrong thing. You can trust me."

He nodded again, thinking the question was, Could he trust her completely? Because regardless of whether his suspicions were right or wrong, if they got back to a certain pair of ears he could kiss his position at Four Corners goodbye.

But did he really have a choice about trusting her? Given the notes?

She might honestly figure they were nothing more than an attempt to scare her off, or she might only have been saying that. Either way, he wasn't convinced it was true.

After all the trouble the saboteur had gone to, was he likely to give up now? Simply because she'd appeared on the scene?

Or would he just be more determined to press on? To do whatever he figured it would take to get the end result he wanted?

Since Noah would bet big money on the latter, he finally said, "Let's get back to your question about who you should pay special attention to."

Dana leaned forward a little.

"For starters, I'd say Chris Vidal."

"The director of logistics," she said. "I haven't met him yet."

"No. I wanted to introduce you to him yesterday, but he was off somewhere until late afternoon."

"And you think he might be our man because…?"

"It's all circumstantial."

"Well, there's nothing wrong with circumstantial—despite what the movies imply. Sometimes you can build a very strong case with it."

"Okay, you know more or less what Chris does for us?"

"Basically. Your uncle gave me copies of the key job descriptions. The director of logistics is responsible for all the details involved in getting the collectibles from their sources to your clients. Right?"

"Right," Noah said, reflecting that Chris would be royally put out if he heard his job summarized in such simplistic terms.

Half the time *he* talked about it, he portrayed himself as a miracle worker.

Of course, some of those job descriptions were pretty bare-bones, so he said, "Maybe I should elaborate a little. Then it'll be easier for you to see what's made me suspicious of him."

When Dana nodded, he continued.

"For everything Robert sources, Chris starts by deciding on the best method of shipping. Then he chooses the specific company to use, deals with all the import and export regulations, the Customs forms, the duty payments and any other red tape that gets in our way.

"Some of the things we acquire go directly from their country of origin to our clients. But the majority come through our warehouse, which means that Chris works closely with Stu Refkin and his men."

He could see Dana's level of interest notch up as he told her that.

"He knows what's in the warehouse at any given

moment, and when the staff will have to be working overtime.''

''Or, alternatively,'' she said, ''when it would be safe to sneak in and set a fire? Or rig a stack of crates?''

''Exactly.''

''And he'd have known how and when those missing containers were supposed to arrive.''

''You catch on quick.''

She smiled. ''That's why I'm a world-renowned P.I. What you haven't told me, though, is whether Chris has a key to the warehouse.''

''Not officially. But he's around there often enough that he could easily have had the chance to 'borrow one to copy' as you put it.''

''Since the locks were changed after the fire, he'd have had to do it twice,'' she pointed out.

''Yeah, that's the weak link.''

''Of course, if he did it once he *might* have done it again,'' Dana said, not sounding entirely convinced. ''Especially if one of the fellows there usually leaves his keys lying around.''

''I haven't seen that, and I've been keeping my eyes open. But getting back to the question of who else might have learned who you really are, Chris is seriously into computers. So if he figured there was something fishy when he got Robert's memo about you, he could have checked you out even faster than I did.

''Plus, something you told me points to him.''

"What?"

"You said the second note wasn't put in your brief-case until after your meeting with Robert. And that didn't end until quite a bit after five, did it?"

"No."

"Well, Chris was still around then. I saw him while I was waiting for you."

"Waiting so you could follow me."

"Ah…yeah."

She smiled once more. "We won't get into that again because you've just redeemed yourself. I have a feeling you might really be on to something here."

He tried not to show how much her thinking he could be right pleased him.

"Is Chris in today?" she asked. "Could you intro-duce me to him as soon as we get back?"

"Yeah, he should be there."

"Good."

"Order's up, Noah," Roxy called over.

When Dana reached for her purse, he said, "My treat."

"Then it's my turn next time."

"Deal."

He rose, liking the promise of a next time. He also liked the fact that their conversation had gone far bet-ter than he'd hoped.

Not only did Dana figure Chris was a viable pos-sibility, but if she was going to be busy with him this afternoon there was little reason to tell her about his *other* suspect just yet. It could wait.

And hell, if this was really his lucky day, she'd drag a confession out of Chris. Then there'd be no reason to tell her at all.

His buoyant mood lasted until they arrived back at Four Corners and found Chris in his office, but it quickly began to fade once he'd introduced Dana and it was time for him to get going.

"So," he made himself say. "I'll leave you two to talk."

He took a reluctant step backward; his feet refused to take a second one.

Until recently, he'd never thought about Chris Vidal being anything other than what he seemed—a young man on his way up, with a real talent for logistics.

Now, not only did he suspect that Chris was the saboteur, he'd begun to worry about his being mentally unbalanced. Because surely those notes weren't the product of a sane mind.

So was it really a good idea for Dana to be on her own with someone who could well be dangerous? Of course it wasn't.

"I'll check in with you later, Noah," she said. Then she smiled across Chris's desk at him.

As Chris smiled back, Noah's stomach lurched.

He had no talent for figuring out whether or not another man was the type women found attractive. But that warm smile of Dana's made him assume Chris was.

And he sure didn't want her getting too friendly with the guy when he could be...

Even if he wasn't...

Hell, the bottom line was that he didn't want her getting too friendly with another man. No other man. Which was downright ridiculous.

He barely knew the woman. Well...actually, that wasn't true any longer.

By this point he knew she was intelligent. And had a quirky sense of humor. Along with a subtle sexiness that made his throat a little dry every time he looked at her.

But setting those things aside, he'd never been the jealous type. So what on earth had him standing here thinking he wanted Dana Morancy completely to himself?

Especially when he wasn't even remotely close to having her at all—let alone to himself.

It was just occurring to him that *he* might be becoming mentally unbalanced, when she caught his eye and gave him a pointed gaze that said to get out and close the door.

He forced himself to do so, then stood staring at it, wishing he had X-ray vision.

CHAPTER TEN

AFTER NOAH HAD CLOSED the door, Dana gave Chris Vidal another smile and said, "I assume you're clear on what my assignment here is all about?"

He nodded, not looking even marginally at ease, so she added, "Does something about it bother you?"

"That depends."

"Oh? On what?"

"I guess on whether or not Robert's been straight with me. Not that he normally isn't," Chris added quickly, clearly afraid she'd be repeating every word he said.

"It's just...well, I asked him about you after I got his All Staff memo. Frankly, I was afraid he and Larry weren't happy with the job I've been doing, that I was part of the reason they hired you."

"You weren't," she assured him. "Not that I'm aware of, at least. In fact, everything I've heard about you so far—which admittedly isn't much—has been positive."

That made him seem less uneasy.

"But what started you thinking they might have concerns?"

"Well, I figured they could be holding me responsible for those cargo containers going astray."

"Why you?"

He shrugged. "Because they'd used the same shipping line for years, but I'd been having problems with it so I decided to try a different company—which wasn't one of my better decisions.

"Nothing the old line had done wrong even came close to completely losing part of a shipment."

She nodded, as if commiserating, while wondering if his "different company" was one he'd known did things like stealing cargo containers.

Next, she wondered what his share of the take would have been.

Since she could hardly ask him about that, though, she said, "Stu Refkin's worried that they're blaming *him*."

"Stu? Never. The bosses know he's the last guy in the world who makes mistakes. Besides, they're aware it was Tony Zicco who screwed up."

"Oh?"

Chris looked at her as if he figured there was no way she hadn't already heard the details, but proceeded to provide them, anyway.

"Tony didn't check the delivery form against the shipment. If he had, we wouldn't have ended up short."

"So there are flaws in the warehouse receiving system," she said in her best OD jargon.

"I'd say there's a flaw in Tony."

She waited, hoping Chris would elaborate.

When a few seconds passed and he didn't, she said, "You mean he's generally not careful enough?"

Chris shrugged. "I spend a lot of time with the warehouse guys. Stu and Paul are totally reliable. Tony...

"Well, you get my drift. But it's only my opinion, and I'd just as soon you didn't tell anyone I expressed it."

"Absolutely," she said. "I appreciate your mentioning it, though. After all, my job is to determine where the rough edges are and suggest ways of smoothing them out."

"Well, Tony's definitely a rough edge."

But was he more than that? Could he be their man? Despite her feeling that it wasn't any of the warehouse people?

There was no subtle way of pressing Chris, so she finally said, "Why don't you tell me about your role in the company. And about anything, internally speaking, that you think might improve the way it runs."

Chris nodded, then launched into a detailed explanation of what a logistics person did.

Dana half listened to him and half considered what he'd had to say about the warehouse workers.

Aside from Larry Benzer, who was convinced that one, two or all of them must be involved in the sabotage, everybody she'd talked with thus far seemed to hold Stu Refkin in high esteem.

She knew very little about Paul Coulter yet—except that he'd never laid a hand on that delivery form.

As for Tony Zicco, there was no disputing the fact he'd slipped up. The unknown was whether it had been accidental or intentional.

Accidental…accident. Her thoughts went scurrying to what had happened this morning.

Would Tony have rigged that crate to fall and then positioned himself so he'd be the victim? Just in case anyone was suspicious of him?

She simply didn't know. It would have been an extreme and risky move, yet it was amazing what people sometimes did. But the fact remained that all three of the warehouse men had sailed through their lie detector tests.

She turned her full attention back to Chris Vidal—then almost immediately realized she was comparing him with Noah.

Not tall and dark, but medium height, with light brown, almost blond hair and blue eyes. As for handsome, that was a definite yes, although he didn't ring her chimes.

He put her a little in mind of a young Robert Redford, whereas Noah reminded her of…

Actually, Noah didn't remind her of anyone. Noah Haine was…

She searched for the right word.

Unique? Special? Extraordinary?

When *extremely sexy* snuck onto her list she reminded herself for the millionth time that the man was off-limits.

Then she made herself feel better by adding *for the moment.*

TRY AS HE MIGHT, Noah couldn't keep his mind on the work in front of him.

He was too busy worrying about what might be going on in Chris Vidal's office. Despite being almost certain that, even if Chris was their saboteur, he wouldn't try anything right here and now.

Finally, he gave up on attempting to concentrate and headed for the second floor—to see if Dana's lock had been fixed yet.

Once he reached the upstairs reception area, he could see that Helen, the only one around, was eating a late lunch at her desk.

Fleetingly, he thought about what Dana had said. That it would have been easy for Helen to slip in and print those notes. And here was proof of it. All alone, nobody to observe what she was doing…

But that was crazy. She was *not* the one. He'd bet the bank on it.

"You work too hard," he greeted her.

"I know. And I wish you'd tell Robert and Larry that the next time you're talking money. I could use a raise."

"I'll keep it in mind. Has the locksmith been yet?"

"Uh-huh. He did the front and alley doors and

fixed that lock for Dana. He just headed for the warehouse a few minutes ago.''

''Good.''

''He left the keys with me. Here's your new master,'' she added, opening a drawer and taking it out. ''And if you see Dana tell her I've got hers.''

The locksmith had left the keys with Helen. The new masters—which he, Robert and Larry weren't going to let out of their sight.

But if Helen *was* the one, she might already have had a copy made. That ''few minutes ago'' could easily have been half an hour.

Telling himself again that she was *not* the one, he stuck the key into his pocket. He was about to head back downstairs when she said, ''Noah?''

''Yeah?''

She glanced around, as if assuring herself they really were alone, then said, ''Is it okay if I ask you something that's none of my business?''

''Sure, as long as it's okay if I decide not to answer.''

''This isn't a joke. It's *really* none of my business.''

''Well…okay, try me anyway.''

She hesitated, clearly uneasy, but said at last, ''Is your uncle's marriage okay?''

Wondering where on earth that was coming from, he said, ''As far as I know. Why?''

''Because I barely survived his first divorce, so if

there's going to be a second one I want time to gear up for it.''

"Ah," he said, for lack of anything better to say.

"Or I might just quit."

"You aren't serious." At least, he sure hoped she wasn't. She was virtually indispensable.

"Well, I'm serious about not wanting to go through anything like that again. He used to come in here every day looking more miserable than you'd believe. Especially considering *he* was the one who'd found somebody new."

Noah could see Helen expected a response to that, but he didn't know what to say.

He'd been in high school when Robert's first marriage broke up, which put it at least fifteen or sixteen years ago. He hadn't forgotten the details, though, and Helen was right. Robert *had* found somebody new. And he'd married Carol practically the day after the divorce was final.

His mother's reaction to the situation was another thing Noah hadn't forgotten.

Her outrage, when she'd learned that her brother-in-law was leaving his wife for another woman, had been something else.

After all this time, she'd pretty much accepted Carol as family. But back then she'd gone days without speaking to his father—for refusing to sit down with Robert and have a brotherly talk.

By which she'd meant, as she'd put it, "You've

got to tell Robert he has to think with his brain instead of his Johnson.''

He shifted his mind back to the present as Helen gave up on him saying anything and began speaking again.

''The only time he didn't have a hangdog expression,'' she was saying, ''was when Carol came by to go for lunch with him. Then his face would light up and…''

Shaking her head, she left it at that and once again sat waiting for a response.

This time he figured he'd better give her one, so he said, ''If Robert and Carol are having problems I don't know about them. But what makes you think they might be?''

''Dana,'' she said.

''Dana?'' he repeated uncertainly.

Helen nodded. ''Something's going on there.''

''What do you mean, going on?''

''Robert's…I don't know quite how to put it, but he's somehow fascinated by her.''

''Fascinated?'' Hell, he was sounding like a parrot, but what—precisely—was Helen getting at?

''Uh-huh. The way I've seen him looking at her. And his body language when he's talking to her. There's something about it…''

''I haven't noticed anything.''

Her expression said, *Naturally not, you're a man.*

What she said aloud was ''Well, I've probably seen them interacting more than you. And it's very subtle.

But after thirty years of working for Robert and Larry I know both of them almost as well as my husband.

"And I asked about Robert's marriage because the way he's acting has me remembering when Carol was his girlfriend."

Noah almost said "girlfriend?" but swallowed it.

"The way he used to talk to her..." Helen continued. "It's not *exactly* the same as that, but it's the closest I can come to explaining."

"You mean he's..." He rejected *in love,* because that would be absurd given the short time Robert had known Dana, and went with "You're saying he's infatuated with her?"

Helen shrugged. "If that *is* it, he must be having a midlife crisis. She's young enough to be his daughter. But...when you get to thinking, there are a whole lot of strange things about her being here.

"First off, we both know how the bosses view consultants. Hiring one was totally out of character."

She gave him time to nod, then went on.

"And I'll tell you something else. I'm sure Larry doesn't really want her around. No matter what they've said, she's here solely because Robert does.

"And how did he happen to choose *her,* specifically? Did he tell you?"

"No," Noah said, his thoughts reeling. "But if he...*feels* something for her, do you think she's aware of it? I mean...is it a two-way thing?"

Surely that couldn't be the case, yet Helen looked as if she figured it was a possibility.

"I don't know," she said at last. "I can read him and there's definitely *something* on his side of the equation. But I've barely met her."

Shrugging again, she added, "I probably should have kept quiet. Only I thought you might…

"But if you say things are fine between him and Carol, then my imagination's probably just been working overtime."

"Yeah, maybe that's it." Or maybe not.

Of course, Helen didn't know Dana wasn't actually a consultant. And the fact she was a P.I. explained why she'd been hired. But how *had* Robert chosen her, specifically?

There must be hundreds of investigators in New York. So why her?

Because there *was* something going on between them? Or because Robert was hoping to *start* something? Even though, as Helen had said, he was old enough to be her father?

Had the man taken leave of his senses?

Feeling more than a little stunned, Noah mumbled a "See you later" and started away, his mind returning to something that had skittered through it while Helen had been speaking.

Given the brief time his uncle had known Dana, he couldn't possibly be *in love* with her. Could he?

Noah wasn't a believer in love at first sight. Or second, for that matter. Yet the very first moment *he'd* seen her, he'd felt…

But that had been nothing more than instantaneous

animal attraction. It was only later, after he'd gotten to know her a little...

Well, at this point he'd admit to feeling... He certainly couldn't deny there was a spark. Maybe even a flame. However, he was a million miles away from being in love with the woman.

He paused halfway down the stairs and considered that. If it was true, why did he seem to be constantly thinking about her? And why had his heart done a flash-freeze when he'd seen that smile she'd given Chris?

All right, then. So it wasn't a million miles. Maybe it was only a thousand. But that was still a long way from being in love.

He simply...well, he liked her. And he was physically drawn to her. That was the extent of it.

As for Robert...

When he let his thoughts drift to what might be going on there, they ended up at a question.

Could Robert have known Dana for longer than he was letting on? Was *that* how he'd come to choose her?

If so...hell, if so there was no telling precisely *what* their relationship was.

An unsettled feeling began crawling around in his chest, not unlike the one he'd felt when he'd left Dana alone with Chris.

Before he had time to consider the ramifications of that his uncle materialized at the bottom of the staircase and started up.

Taking his appearance as a sign, Noah said, "Got time to talk?"

"Sure."

He reversed course, heading back upstairs and into Robert's office—studiously ignoring the conspiratorial look Helen gave him.

As he closed the door, Robert said, "What's up?"

Reminding himself he wasn't supposed to know the truth about Dana, he said, "Oh, I'm just wondering what our consultant's hearing from people. Has she learned anything that's got you zeroing in on a suspect?"

"Not yet. But I don't think we should expect too much too fast. It'll take her a while to get a real sense of the company. And for people to feel comfortable talking to her."

"Yeah. I guess. But you're still hopeful she'll turn up something? Something that'll help us?"

Robert smiled. "You know me, Noah. I'm always an optimist."

"Uh-huh," he said, racking his brain for a subtle way to ask the next question.

Since he couldn't come up with one, he straight out said, "How did you choose her, anyway? Was she someone Martha Benzer had heard of?"

"No, Martha was only pushing the general idea of an OD person. But you seem uneasy about Dana. Do you think there's a problem with her?"

"No, not at all. I only—"

"Good, because as consultants go she strikes me

as pretty competent. So let's not worry about how she's making out until she's had more time.''

"Yeah, you're probably right."

Robert nodded. "She came highly recommended. And she mentioned having a knack for knowing when people are lying. Said her father's a cop and he taught her the trick of it when she was just a kid."

"Ah."

"So, all in all, I think we've got ourselves not only an OD consultant but an amateur detective. She even named her cat Dr. Watson. You know? Sherlock Holmes's sidekick?''

Noah manufactured a smile, but he was having a tough time keeping a lid on his anger. The way Robert was stringing him along—or believed he was, at least—was downright infuriating.

"So I really *am* hopeful she'll pick up on something that'll point us in the right direction," he added.

"Yeah. Maybe she will. Although I *still* think you'd have been smarter to hire a *real* detective."

Robert didn't look even marginally rattled by that remark, and after a few seconds of silence he said, "Was there something else?"

Now what? He could hardly ask his married uncle whether he had the hots for a woman half his age.

"Noah?"

"No. Nothing else. As I said, I was just wondering if she'd heard anything of interest."

"Well, when she does I'll certainly tell you."

"*When.* Positive thinking. That's good." He turned

and walked back out of the office, mouthing the word *nothing* to Helen on his way by. Then he started down the stairs a second time.

That had taken him absolutely nowhere. So he'd have to see if he could get further with Dana. But exactly what was he going to ask her?

HER DAILY MEETING with Robert finished, Dana was in her own office putting on her sneakers for the walk home when she got the sense that someone was watching her.

Sure enough, Larry Benzer was standing in the hall outside her doorway.

She smiled over at him, surprised that such a big man could have walked down the hall so quietly she hadn't heard a sound.

"I know it's after five," he said. "If you have a minute, though…"

"Yes, of course."

He stepped into the office, closed the door and lowered himself into one of the visitors' chairs before saying, "How's it going?"

"Things are moving along," she said, wondering if she'd misread him.

Maybe he hadn't simply gone along with hiring a P.I. because Robert had wanted to. Maybe he was more interested in what she was doing than she'd figured.

"I keep thinking about what happened to Tony Zicco this morning," he said.

She nodded. "The only good thing is that it wasn't worse."

"Well, it was bad enough. He called Stu a few hours ago, after they'd finished with him at the hospital. And he's going to be off work for a while."

"Yes, Robert was just telling me that."

Larry eyed her, obviously waiting for her to say something more.

Since Noah had already talked to him about the incident, she doubted there was really anything she could add. But she had to say something, so she went with "I guess Noah told you it certainly wasn't an accident."

"Uh-huh. And isn't that just another thing that says our troublemaker *has* to be one of those guys? Although I guess we can eliminate Tony at this point."

Obviously, just as she'd assumed, Larry was even more convinced his theory was right than he'd already been. So despite the fact that she *wasn't* convinced, she chose her words carefully and said, "I certainly haven't ruled out Stu or Paul."

"But I noticed you were around *here* all afternoon. Not at the warehouse."

"Right. As we discussed, I have to talk to everyone in the company."

He leaned forward, making her just a little uneasy. If he'd been a stranger, she'd have read his expression as menacing.

"Everything points to the warehouse men," he said. "And this mess has to get sorted out before anything *else* happens. In other words, fast. So I want you focusing on them.''

She exhaled slowly, reminding herself Larry was one of ''the bosses.''

''I agree with you. The faster I can figure out who the perp is, the better.

''But don't forget that only you and Robert know I'm an investigator. And the first thing a real OD consultant would do is get a thorough overview of the business. Not zoom straight in on one department and put it under a microscope.''

''I doubt either of those two know what a real OD consultant would do,'' Larry muttered.

''Well, it isn't hard to find out. And they aren't stupid. So if one of them *is* our guy, and he starts to suspect I'm not really a consultant, he'll be doing everything he can to keep me from getting at the truth.''

Larry didn't take even a second to think about that, simply said, ''What if you went through the warehouse very carefully when nobody else was there? I could let you in after hours and you might find something. A clue. Maybe even proof.''

Before she could say a word, he went on. ''I pretty much know the security guard's routine. I could easily let you in while he's on one of the other piers. Then you could snoop around to your heart's content—with no risk of anyone finding out about it.''

''That's certainly worth considering,'' she said slowly. ''Does Robert think it's a good idea?''

"I haven't mentioned it to him. And I don't intend to."

When all she said was "Ah," Larry added, "Look, it must be obvious to you that Robert and I are viewing this problem differently.

"For whatever reason, he's convinced himself that none of the warehouse men are involved. And he's being…

"I have no idea why, but he's being very defensive about them. And he can be damned stubborn at times, so if I ran the idea by him he just might object. But you don't need his approval of everything you do before you do it."

Oh, Lord. She hated assignments where there wasn't one single person in charge.

Again, she chose her words carefully. "It isn't that I have to, but I imagine he told you he's asked me to update him every day?"

"Uh-huh."

"Well, the thing is, I wouldn't feel comfortable doing something like that and then telling him about it after the fact."

Larry clearly didn't like that, so she quickly said, "How about if I talk to both Paul Coulter and Tony Zicco tomorrow."

"Tony won't be here."

"I know, but I'll call him, ask if I can see him at his apartment.

"Given what happened, and that people have been told I'm here because of the problems, I don't think it would really raise any suspicions if I checked up on the latest one.

"As for searching the warehouse, let me mull over the idea for a day or two, all right?"

"I don't see what's to mull."

"I need time to think about what *sort* of clue could be there, aside from anything else."

"Oh. I was figuring something might just jump out at you."

"That usually only happens on TV."

She gave him a smile, but he didn't return it. He merely pushed himself out of the chair, saying, "You tell me when you want in there, then. But keep in mind that we hired you to find the perp. And the longer it takes the more it's going to cost us.

"So as you said yourself, the faster you figure out who he is the better."

CHAPTER ELEVEN

DÉJÀ VU. JUST AS IT HAD yesterday, 5:45 found Noah lurking near the front door.

Following his unproductive chat with Robert, he'd kept an eye on Chris's office, intending to catch Dana as soon as the two of them were finished. After that, or so he'd assumed, things would unfold in a predictable fashion.

She'd fill him in on what their director of logistics had had to say. Then he'd find out, one way or another, whether there *was* anything going on between her and his uncle.

However, his assumptions and reality had parted company once she'd appeared.

She'd said she *really* wanted him to introduce her to the employees she hadn't yet met. And to do it before her four-thirty with Robert. So, thus far, there hadn't been an opportunity for any private discussion.

But he had no intention of letting her escape today. If she didn't want a ride home he'd damned well walk with her.

Pacing along the hallway toward his office once more, he turned his thoughts back to just exactly how he was going to ease into the subject of her relationship with Robert.

No matter what he said, she probably wouldn't like it. So mentioning that Helen had tipped him off wasn't in the cards.

If Dana got annoyed, it might as well only be with him. But if he could figure out a way of asking *without* annoying her…

What he needed was a brilliant idea; he still didn't have one by the time he heard her coming down the stairs.

"Just happen to be here again?" she teased when she saw him.

He smiled, although he was hardly in a smiling mood.

"Thought I could drive you home," he said.

She glanced at her sneakers, then looked at him once more.

"We need to talk," he told her.

"Well…"

"What's wrong?"

"Nothing, really. It's just that leaving together is hardly being circumspect.

"Although, I guess…Larry was in Robert's office talking to him when I started downstairs."

"Come on, then. We'll be gone before they're done. And there's no one else left to see us."

Hoping Noah was right, Dana followed him through the silence of the building and out into the heat of the alley—where three cars were pulled up with their noses practically touching the brick wall.

"That's mine," he said, motioning toward the midnight-blue Lexus.

When he opened the doors he might as well have been opening an oven.

"We'd better give it time to cool down," he suggested.

"No, let's get going."

The other cars had to be Robert's and Larry's, and one of them might walk out at any second.

Noah didn't look happy, but he climbed in and started the engine.

"Good thing I've got an 'arctic' setting," he said, switching the air conditioner to full blast as he backed into the alley.

She began breathing more easily after they'd pulled away. Having one of "the bosses" see Noah driving her home wouldn't be the end of the world, but she'd rather avoid it.

"So." He glanced over at her. "I need a lot of updating. How about beginning with your impression of Chris."

"Well, he told me enough about the logistics of getting things from place A to place B that I could probably take over his job."

Noah shot her one of his great smiles, which reminded her she never *had* put much effort into developing immunity to them.

And now, even if she tried, it would undoubtedly

be too late. Her resolve to keep things platonic, until her work at Four Corners was done, had already weakened considerably.

Weakened, though, was hardly the same as destroyed. Which meant that as long as this job didn't last too long, and if she could avoid spending too much time with Noah before it was done...

He'd begun speaking, and she tuned in as he was saying that Chris was always more than eager to talk about his work.

"But aside from that what did you think?" he concluded. "Could he be our man?"

"Well, if I'd met him cold I probably wouldn't have suspected him at all. After what you told me, though..."

"See?" he said, giving her another smile. "I was right. We're better off working together."

Together. The combination of that word and his smile sent a tiny ripple of desire through her.

She did her best to ignore it, but her best wasn't very good. She could practically see another few threads of her resolve unraveling.

"He didn't say anything even marginally incriminating?" Noah added.

"Uh-uh. But *whoever's* behind this is smart. He won't make things easy for us."

"No, I guess not."

Noah edged into the traffic on Tenth, then began inching his way north before he asked, "How was your meeting with Robert?"

"Okay."

"Only okay?"

She glanced across the car at his even profile, something in his tone warning her that question wasn't as casual as he'd tried to make it sound.

Since she didn't have any idea why it shouldn't be, she said, "Do you know something I don't?"

"No. Your 'okay' just didn't seem very happy."

"Oh. Well…it's nothing serious. Only that I'm not used to reporting in to a client every day and I'm finding it a bit awkward."

When Noah looked at her again, she said, "The problem's that I can tell Robert hopes I'll say I'm making great progress. That I already have a specific suspect in mind. Whereas I don't want to get ahead of myself.

"If I start him thinking it's one person and it turns out to be someone else…"

"Ah. Right. But if you aren't saying much, then my uncle sure must be doing a lot of talking. I mean, you're in his office an awfully long time."

"Actually, today I'm so late because I was talking to Larry after I finished with Robert. Or, more accurately, *he* was talking to *me*. That's a whole *other* story."

"Oh?"

Before she could get into it, a cell phone began to ring.

"It's mine," Noah said as she reached toward her

briefcase. "But I'll let the voice mail take it. Let's hear what Larry wanted."

Quickly, she filled him in, thinking that the more she told him the less he seemed to like what she was saying.

"This letting you into the warehouse," he said when she was done. "Exactly what does he have in mind? The two of you in there, together, in the middle of the night?"

"I'm not really sure. He said *let* me in, so *I* could look around. But he might be thinking he'd help me with it.

"He'd certainly want to lock up when I was done. And make sure I didn't leave at the wrong time—while the security guard's patroling your pier. So I guess maybe he does figure on staying there with me.

"Why? Is there something I should know? Like he's liable to come on to me?"

Noah slowly shook his head, looking worried, yet what he said was "I really doubt he'd do that. Martha can be difficult, but he's crazy about her. Besides, if he ever fooled around she'd serve him his... Well, she's not the sort of woman who'd put up with that, and he knows it."

"Yet you don't think I should go along with his warehouse idea."

"No."

"Why? Because it's sneaky? I'm afraid that some-times goes with my job."

"Yeah, but... It bothers me, that's all."

When she said "Why?" again, he shrugged. "I guess I've just been having a lot of trouble with the way Larry's...

"He doesn't normally go at anything like a dog at a bone. But he just won't shut up when it comes to the warehouse guys. And since neither you nor I nor Robert really figures it *is* one of them..."

"We *could* all be wrong."

"Yeah, we could."

"Well, I still have to talk to both Paul Coulter and Tony Zicco. Maybe, if we *are* wrong, one of them will say something that...

"At any rate, I promised Larry I'd try to see both of them tomorrow."

"You're assuming Tony won't mind when he's off sick?"

"I'm hoping he won't, because it'll make Larry happier—kind of a trade-off for my not being gung-ho about his search suggestion."

They made their way another half block or so before Noah said, "We left something hanging. Why are your meetings with Robert lasting so long?"

"Well, he..."

She hesitated, wary of elaborating, fearful that Noah might repeat what she said. Which, when she thought about it, was pretty ironic.

After all, only this morning he'd expressed concern that *she'd* slip up—say something to make Robert and Larry realize he'd been sleuthing without filling them in about it. Or realize that he'd learned her true identity and was keeping the fact a secret from them.

But he'd decided to trust her. And even though he'd dragged her into this partnership unwillingly...

"He what?" Noah asked, interrupting her thoughts.

"Pardon?"

"You started to explain about the meetings, but you didn't get very far."

"Oh. Yes. Well, it's just that Robert's...friendlier than most of my clients."

"Friendlier."

"Uh-huh. Both yesterday and today, after I finished telling him what I'd been doing, he obviously wanted to chat. It's almost as if he's lonely, which I'm sure he's not."

She gazed at Noah, waiting for his response.

"You're right," he said at last. "Robert has his wife. A lot of friends. I can't imagine he's lonely, but...I want to ask you something."

"What?"

"When did he first get in touch with you?"

"Last week."

"That was the very first you met him?"

"Yes. He came to my office on Wednesday. Why?"

The traffic had completely stopped moving, so Noah was able to give her a long, appraising look. It made her absolutely certain he was trying to figure out whether or not she was telling the truth.

Then he nodded, almost imperceptible, but enough to suggest he'd decided he believed her.

"He just showed up at your office or...?"

She shook her head, not at all sure where this was going. "He'd made an appointment beforehand."

"And why did he choose *you?* Did you ask him?"

"Noah, what are you trying to get at?"

"It made him choose you, as opposed to some other investigator."

"But why do you care?"

When he didn't reply, she said, "Okay. I asked who'd referred him to me and he said it was a police officer I used to work with. But he couldn't give me the name because someone else had done the legwork. Now, tell me why you're asking all these questions."

"I was just curious."

She didn't buy that for a second.

"Noah, we agreed not to hold anything back. Ground rule number one, remember?"

He stared at the lines of cars idling in front of them, saying nothing.

Then, when she was almost about to press him, he turned toward her again and said, "There's something funny about the way Robert acts around you."

That took her by surprise.

"Funny?" she said. "Funny how?"

"I can't quite put my finger on it. But he's different with you than he usually is."

"Because I'm a P.I. It throws some people."

"Well, almost nothing throws my uncle, so I'd say it has to be something else."

"What?"

"I'm not sure."

After thinking for a moment, she said, "You've barely seen me with him."

"I've seen enough to know there's something funny."

The traffic began moving again.

Noah turned his attention back to his driving, leaving her wondering if he was right. If Robert actually *was* acting out-of-character around her. And if so, why.

RATHER THAN JUST STOPPING to let Dana out, Noah pulled into a parking space down the block from her building. That made her fairly sure he'd like an invitation in, and he confirmed her suspicion by cutting the ignition.

She tried to think of an excuse for not asking him up.

Given the weakened state of her resolve, being alone with him in her apartment probably wouldn't be wise.

Before a believable excuse came to mind he leveled a warm gaze at her—and she knew there was no "probably" about it.

"It's a little early to eat yet," he said. "So why don't we spend some time talking about the people at Four Corners. Then we can go someplace for dinner.

"All strictly business," he added, apparently guessing she might well say no.

"The more we talk, the more likely I'll tell you something that'll strike a spark. Right?"

"Yes, but—"

"Besides, I want to meet Dr. Watson."

He smiled, as if that clinched his case. Instead, it gave her a distinctly unsettled feeling. How did he know her cat's name?

When she asked, he said, "Robert mentioned it."

"Oh? Did he also mention how he knew it?"

Noah seemed puzzled. "I assumed from you."

"Uh-uh. And why on earth was he talking about my cat?"

"He wasn't. Not really. But we were talking about you and—"

"Talking *what* about me?"

"Just…talking. Basically, I was trying to find out why he's acting funny.

"*Subtly* trying," he elaborated as she gave him a look to say that sounded risky.

"And he was telling me your father's a cop… Is that true, by the way?"

"Yes."

"Ah. Does it explain why you became one?"

"Likely. Mostly, at least."

She was searching for something to say that would

get them off *that* subject when Noah said, "We really don't know much about each other, do we."

She shook her head, thinking that wasn't an ideal topic, either.

Not that she wasn't interested in learning more about him. Far from it. But if they could just avoid discussing personal things until after—

"I think we should fill in a few of the blanks," he said. "Since we're partners and all."

She considered pointing out that personal details hardly fell into the "strictly business" arena, but Noah was already saying, "I grew up in a big old house on Long Island. My parents still live in it.

"I've got two younger sisters, one who's married and has a couple of little boys. The other's a teacher. She lives on the Upper West Side—with a prosecuting attorney my father can't stand."

He stopped there and waited for her to take a turn.

"Only child," she told him.

"And?"

"And I grew up in Queens. My dad's still in the house there, but he's on his own. My mom died three years ago."

"Ah. Sorry," he said quietly.

She nodded, then said, "Could we go back to how Doc got into your conversation with Robert?"

"You don't want to hear more about me?" he said with such an exaggerated hurt-feelings expression that she couldn't help but smile.

"Of course I do," she told him. "First, though, I

want to figure out how Robert knew about my cat. So exactly what did he say?''

"Well, he made a comment to the effect that you seemed to have inherited some *amateur* detective genes from your father."

"Amateur," she repeated.

"Right. I'd probably have thought it was pretty funny if I hadn't been so annoyed that he was lying to me.

"At any rate, that's what led into the bit about the cat's name."

She uneasily licked her lips. "I recall telling him my dad's a cop, but I'm virtually certain I didn't say anything about Doc."

"You must have. How else would he even know you have a cat, let alone what it's called?"

Good question. She racked her brain, trying to remember every word she'd ever said to Robert.

That was impossible to do, of course. They'd had several lengthy conversations. So maybe there'd been a throwaway line that she hadn't thought a thing about at the time.

Focusing on Noah again, she said, "Do you think I'm old enough to be having memory lapses?"

He laughed. "That must be it. But where are we going from here? Meeting the cat? Talking about the company's employees? Catching some dinner. Sound like a good plan?"

Even thought she had grave doubts as to the "good" part, he'd been right about one thing. The more they talked, the more likely he'd say something that would give her a lead.

With that in mind, she reluctantly nodded.

It earned her another of his devastating smiles—which only reinforced her fear that she was skating on extremely thin ice.

DOC CAME CHARGING from the bedroom when Dana opened her apartment door—ready to launch into his full greeting routine until he discovered she wasn't alone.

He stopped dead, narrowed his eyes and began twitching his tail.

"Hey, there you are." Noah crouched down, slowly extending his hand.

Dana set her briefcase on the floor and started unlacing her sneakers, saying, "It takes him a while to warm up to strangers."

She barely got the words out before Doc began edging forward. He didn't stop until he was near enough to cautiously sniff Noah's fingers.

"Good cat," he murmured.

Doc eased another inch closer.

"Good cat," Noah repeated, brushing his knuckles across the soft gray fur of Doc's head.

"He likes me," he said while Doc pushed against his hand, demanding more.

She nodded, thinking she shouldn't be surprised to learn the man's animal magnetism worked on real *animals,* not just on her.

"My mother's a cat person," he told her. "There were always a couple in the house when I was growing up."

"Oh? I've never had one before, so this guy's given me some unexpected moments. And the first time he pounced on me during the night he almost gave me a heart attack."

Noah grinned; she could practically hear that thin ice cracking.

"Mind if I take off my jacket?" he said, pushing himself up from the floor.

"No, go ahead."

Even though she knew it was a bad idea, she watched him shrug out of it.

Like his suit, his shirt had to be tailor-made. It clung perfectly to the muscles of his broad shoulders and the firm wall of his chest.

As he loosened his tie and undid his top button, she had an almost irresistible urge to lick her lips.

Not good, she warned herself. Not *at all* good.

He draped his jacket over the end of the couch, then glanced at her expectantly.

"Would you like coffee or something?" she offered.

"How about a glass of water?"

She headed for the kitchen, very aware of him trailing casually after her.

"I like your place," he said as she reached into the fridge for the water jug.

"Thanks."

Before shutting the door she took a deep breath of the cold air—but it did nothing to cool her blood.

She doubted anything could.

Not with him standing so close that his body heat was warming her. Not with the faint, sultry fragrance of his cologne making her think of forbidden sex.

The scent smelled expensive. The way his clothes looked. And his car.

Noah Haine wasn't only a gorgeous man, he was a successful one, as well.

He'd probably never made a serious mistake in his entire career.

Nothing that would even come close to rivaling the one she'd made. The one that had brought an end to her life on the job. That had almost destroyed her.

Ordering those thoughts from her mind, she set the jug on the counter and turned to get glasses.

"Dana?" he said.

Her mouth went dry. Then she met his dark gaze and it went drier still.

There was desire in his eyes, and merely seeing it started her own desire pooling inside her.

"Uh-huh?" she managed to say.

He slowly rubbed his jaw, his eyes not leaving hers.

For the second time, she was barely able to keep from licking her lips.

It was only too easy to imagine his long fingers rubbing *her* skin—so easy that she could almost feel it tingling beneath his touch.

She forced her gaze from his but couldn't make herself look entirely away from him.

There was something absolutely mesmerizing about the exposed hollow of his throat and the dark chest hairs visible behind the unbuttoned collar of his shirt.

"Look," he said at last. "I'm not forgetting you don't want Robert or Larry to think you'd do the slightest thing that's...*uncircumspect*."

He paused and smiled. "You realize how few women would use that word?"

"It's a good word," she said, trying hard not to let his smile make her brain any mushier than it already was.

"Yeah, I guess it *is* good. But that doesn't mean I like it. Dana, if you and I had met at a party or something..."

Tentatively, he rested the length of his fingers against her cheek—his touch so warm and gentle it almost made her lean into it the way Doc had.

"We didn't, though," she murmured. "Meet at a party or something. So for the time being..."

"Yeah," he said quietly.

He continued gazing at her; she told herself to move away from him.

To get out of range of his body heat, of his sultry male scent.

To take a giant step backward, reach into the cupboard for those glasses, do anything that would shatter the tension between them.

And then it was too late.

CHAPTER TWELVE

NOAH EASED CLOSER and brushed Dana's cheek with a kiss. A barely there kiss she knew was designed to make her want more.

It did. There was no contest between the remnants of her resolve and the need deep in her belly.

But rather than kissing her a second time, he stepped back and simply stood looking at her again.

"You know what I got to thinking after we first met?" he asked.

She swallowed hard—half relieved, half disappointed, then said, "No. What?"

"Well, you were still in Robert's office, talking with him and Larry. And I found myself thinking how amazing it was that a stranger could walk into my life and make such an incredibly strong impression on me."

"Is that what I did?" she murmured, so warm inside that she was probably throwing off heat like a roaring fire.

"Uh-huh. When you walked in the door that morning I took one look at you and wondered if you were married. Then I checked your ring finger and wondered how you couldn't be."

For a second she didn't realize he'd meant that to be a question.

When it dawned on her he had, she said, "There's really nothing much to wonder about. I've just never met a man who seemed quite right for me."

She hesitated, but since she badly wanted to know, added, "And you?"

"I've just never met a man who seemed quite right for me, either."

She laughed, feeling the tension between them ease, then said, "That's not fair. Be serious."

He met her gaze once more and the electricity was back—twice as strong. It raced through her body, igniting each nerve ending as it passed.

"Well," he said slowly, "I guess I'm the sort of man who tends to focus on one thing at a time. First there was college, then grad school, then I was working hard to get my career going. And...

"Marriage has always been something I've thought of in the future tense. Whenever I've gone out with a woman who seemed to be looking for a husband it made me nervous. And I'd back off. Or she'd back off because I wasn't acting committed enough to suit her.

"But... It hasn't been a case of figuring I'd *never* get married and have kids.

"What about you? Do you want children?"

As casually as he'd asked the question, she had the sense there was nothing remotely casual about this conversation—which made her knees just a little weak.

"Uh-huh," she said, doing her best to match his nonchalant tone. "I think kids are great."

He smiled at that, starting her heart hammering so hard the sound almost drowned out what he was saying next. Almost, but not entirely.

"I really like you, Dana," he told her quietly. "Really, really like you."

Moving closer once more, he rested his hands on either side of her face. And then he kissed her.

Warm and slow and lingering. Taking all the time in the universe. His lips lazily making magic with hers.

She kissed him back. It would have been impossible to resist. As impossible as it would have been to stop the kisses from growing more intimate. Moist and seeking. Teasing. Arousing.

She'd never dreamed that kissing *any* man could be like this, could start her entire body reacting to his and make her feel such a dazed longing that everything around them gradually faded into nothingness.

Leaving only Noah. And her. And the simmering heat of desire.

He drew her nearer, welding his length to hers. His erection was pressed against her stomach now and her breasts were crushed to his chest, her nipples hard and craving his touch.

But this was not supposed to happen.

Some tattered vestige of rational thought began whispering that in her ear—and ordering her to stop.

It was the last thing she wanted to do, yet she knew if she didn't she'd only find herself in deeper. So gathering every bit of her willpower she broke the kiss.

However, nothing in the world could have made her draw away from Noah. She simply rested her cheek against his chest and they stood like that, his breath whispering against her hair, his arms still around her, until he finally said, "Dana, I didn't intend that to be quite so..."

"Me, neither," she murmured.

He kissed the top of her head. "There's no reason anyone has to know about us."

Us. He was thinking of them in those terms.

She knew she should remind him the big picture hadn't changed, tell him that *circumspect* was still the word of the hour. Because she wasn't a first-rate actor.

If they let things between them develop the way they were heading, people would be able to tell what was going on merely by looking at her. Yet she couldn't make herself say what she should.

"We can be perfectly businesslike from nine to five," he said. "But on our own time, when we're not at Four Corners... How does that sound?"

Before she could decide what to reply, someone knocked on the door.

"Neighbor?" he asked.

"I don't know. My father dropped by after his shift yesterday, but that was a rarity. He'd never do it two days in a row."

"Then let's ignore whoever's there."

As much as she'd love to do that, to just stay right here in Noah's arms, her brain was working again—maybe not at full capacity, but well enough to make her realize this interruption might have come at a very opportune time.

NOAH REMAINED BEHIND in the kitchen while Dana went to answer the door.

Common sense told him she wouldn't want anyone knowing she had an aroused man in her apartment. And boy, oh boy, was he aroused. Kissing her had been...

Hell, there weren't words to describe it. But it was definitely something he wanted to do again. And again. And again after that. Maybe just keep on doing it forever.

He quickly slapped a lid on that idea. As much as he liked Dana he wasn't looking for a lifetime commitment.

Marriage was *still* something he thought of in the future tense, although he had a hunch the future had been creeping up on him while he wasn't looking.

Even so, he hadn't known her long enough to start contemplating the long term.

On the other hand, he wasn't blind to the fact that the tantalizing way she smelled, the softness of her body against his and those absolutely incredible kisses weren't things any red-blooded man would be able to easily walk away from.

As he heard the locks clicking he moved nearer to the doorway, curious about who'd come calling.

He listened to the sound of the door opening—then his heart lurched when a man said, "Hi, darling."

Darling?

She'd told him she'd never met anyone who seemed quite right for her, yet this guy was obviously on pretty close terms.

"You're a surprise," she was saying.

"Not a bad one, I hope."

"Don't be silly."

The door closed and the man said, "I've been doing a lot of thinking since last night."

Last night? Noah's heart lurched again.

What had *she* been doing last night while *he'd* been sitting at his computer, homing in on her real identity?

"And I've got a few ideas that should be worth kicking around," the man continued. "So I figured it made sense to get together."

"Oh, that's great. The only thing is…"

The only thing is you interrupted my kissing someone else in the kitchen, Noah fantasized she'd say.

And it was incredible, he added. If he was going to fantasize, he might as well do a good job of it.

"I have company" was what she said in reality.

"Oh?" The man didn't sound as if he liked that news flash.

"Noah?" she called. "Come meet my father."

Father. Oh. Well, this was okay, then.

Feeling immensely better, he strode out of the kitchen.

As he did, Dana was saying, "I told you about Noah, remember, Dad? The director of finance of Four Corners? Well, he knows that I'm really a P.I.— which I'll explain about later."

Her father, who was wearing an NYPD uniform, turned and gave Noah an appraising look.

"Noah Haine, my father, Jack Morancy," Dana said.

"Glad to meet you, sir."

Noah smiled and extended his hand. Jack Morancy shook it and smiled back. But *his* smile had an edge to it.

Noah fleetingly glanced at Dana and realized where the problem lay.

The skin on her cheeks and around her mouth was red from whisker burn. Not to mention that her lips were a little swollen from their kissing.

Then he remembered the top button of his shirt was undone. And his loosened tie, he saw when he checked it, was badly wrinkled.

It would be obvious to Jack Morancy that something, or someone, had been pressed tightly enough against it to cause terminal creases in the silk.

He tried not to think about the importance of first impressions while Dana told him that she'd discussed the situation at Four Corners with her father. "In strictest confidence, of course," she concluded.

"Of course."

"Could I speak to you in private?" Morancy said to his daughter.

DOC BEAT A RAPID RETREAT from the bed to beneath it as Dana followed her father into the bedroom.

Apparently even the cat could tell Jack Morancy was extremely perturbed. And she felt sure she knew why.

But she was thirty-one years old, for heaven's sake. How concerned should he be about finding a man in her apartment? Especially when, only last night, he'd tried to line her up with...

The fellow's first name didn't come to her, but she remembered he was Ken Kestler's son.

Her father firmly shut the door, then turned to her and said, "What's going on? I thought Noah Haine was one of your suspects."

"Only at first. And he was never really a serious one. Besides..."

"Besides, what?"

"Well, it's complicated. But as I said, he found out I'm really a P.I. and—"

"He *found out?* I was thinking you'd had to tell him for some reason."

"No. He saw through the cover."

"How?"

She shrugged. "He's smart. At any rate, he's been

trying to learn who's behind things at Four Corners for quite a while. So we decided to team up.''

"What? You go undercover on a job and the next thing you do is team up with some amateur? Who might be the perp?''

"But he's not. I just told you. He was never really a very serious suspect. And I established that he can't possibly be—''

"Can't *possibly,*'' her father interrupted cynically.

"That's right. Can't possibly. Give me a little credit, Dad. I know what I'm doing.''

"I realize that, but...why is he here?''

"We were discussing the company's employees. Brainstorming about who *could* be the saboteur.''

She told herself that wasn't exactly a lie. They'd have gotten around to talking about the case sooner or later.

However, Jack Morancy skewered her with the sort of glare she used to get when she'd lied to him as a teenager.

"When you answered the door,'' he said, "you didn't look as if you'd been *discussing* anything.''

She hesitated, feeling her face growing warm—a ridiculous reaction for an adult woman.

"Dad, I'm a big girl. And Noah's a nice man.''

"A nice man you met when? Yesterday?''

"Last week. Which you already knew. But let's drop this, okay?''

"It just strikes me as foolish,'' he muttered. "Of all the men in New York, you want to get mixed up with an executive in your client's company. One who's his nephew, no less. You know better than that.''

Resisting the urge to tell him this was none of his business, she said, "I don't intend to get *mixed up* with Noah Haine. Not in the immediate future, at least."

Jack Morancy eyed her as if debating whether to ask about the nonimmediate future—then apparently decided against it and said, "Dana...I'm just concerned that you could be making an error in judgment."

An error in judgment.

The phrase started a chill creeping through her— and sent her thoughts racing to the subject she'd done her best to keep them away from all day.

This was July 23. The fifth anniversary of...

She gazed at her father, wondering if he realized the significance of the date.

Her mother would have. She'd have called half a dozen times during the day, had her daughter to the house for dinner and done everything she could to keep things light.

Her father, on the other hand, was the sort of person who truly believed the past was the past. For everyone. So odds were, as far as he was concerned, July 23 was simply another day.

It would never occur to him how much what had happened still bothered her. And she'd never tell him.

He already worried too much about her physical

safety. She didn't want him worrying about her emotional health, as well.

But she really wished he hadn't used that damned phrase.

An error in judgment.

When the words wouldn't stop echoing inside her head, her throat started to burn—while the rest of her was feeling so cold by now that she wanted to hug herself.

She didn't, though.

If she let her father see that he'd upset her as much as he had, he'd feel awful. And there was no point in both of them feeling that way.

"Dad, those ideas you came to kick around?" she managed to say. "I told Noah I'd go out for dinner with him, so I can't just ask him to leave. But if the three of us kicking them around would be okay..."

"You know, I'm not sure how I feel about that," he said slowly. "So why don't you give me a call later. After you get home."

"Sure. If you want."

"Yeah, I think that's a better idea."

He shot her a forced smile, then they headed back out of the bedroom.

Noah was sitting on the couch, looking decidedly ill at ease. He rose the moment they reappeared.

"Well, I've got to run," her father said. "It was nice meeting you, Noah."

"Nice meeting you, sir."

"And I'll talk to you later," he told Dana as she opened the door for him.

"Right. I'll phone you."

While she spoke, her gaze inadvertently flickered to where her briefcase was sitting on the floor in the entrance hall, her SIG still stashed inside.

She forced her eyes from it, then watched her father walk down the hall to the stairs, waiting for him to turn and give her a wave. Once he had, she closed the door, that blasted phrase still echoing away.

An error in judgment.

Four little words. Only a handful of letters. Nothing more.

Sometimes, telling herself that helped—but not today.

Her throat had started to burn again and tears were forming in her eyes.

"Dana?" Noah said from somewhere behind her.

Damn. She'd promised herself that this was the year she would *not* cry.

"Dana?" he repeated, closer now.

She silently swore again. If she cried he'd ask questions she didn't want to answer.

Then he encircled her waist with his arm and turned her toward him—and she just couldn't stop the tears from flowing.

IF DANA WERE ALONE she'd have simply curled up into a ball and cried herself out.

She wasn't alone, though. She was sitting on her

couch in Noah's arms, while he kept telling her everything was going to be okay. Which wasn't true.

She'd never forget what had happened, and that boy's face would haunt her for the rest of her life. But right this minute she had to pull herself together before Noah decided she was a complete basket case.

When she finally managed to stop sobbing, more or less, he eased away a few inches and reached for the box of tissues that had been in the kitchen. She had no recollection of his getting it, but he obviously had.

"What happened?" he asked after she'd blown her nose a dozen times. "Did you have a fight with your father?"

She shook her head, not at all sure she could trust her voice. And even if she could, this wasn't something she wanted to talk about.

Talking didn't help. It only forced her to remember more vividly.

"Then what?" he said softly. "Dana...I care about you. So when something's got you this upset..."

He brushed her cheek with his fingers, saying, "Stray tears." Then he cupped her chin and tilted her head up, forcing her to meet his gaze.

"I look awful," she whispered.

"No, you don't."

"Yes, I do. I always look awful after I've been crying."

"Ah. You cry often?"

"No. Almost never."

"Then why now?"

He let the silence stretch, but finally said, "Hey, have you forgotten we're partners? And rule number one is we can't hold anything back."

"Noah, this has nothing to do with Four Corners."

"Then what does it have to do with? Don't shut me out, okay?"

He leaned closer and kissed her forehead. It almost started her tears flowing anew.

"Maybe I can help," he murmured.

"No. Nobody can help. It's just something I have to cope with."

"Dana…at least give me a chance to try."

Closing her eyes, she considered that. As much as she wanted him to let this drop, she didn't think he would. So maybe her only realistic option was to tell him and get it over with.

"I don't know if I can talk about it without starting to cry again," she said at last.

"I can handle crying. I've got two younger sisters, remember?"

She took a deep breath, then exhaled slowly, screwing up all her courage.

But she really, really, didn't want to get into this with him. Every time she had to relive that day it was pure hell.

"Dana?" he said gently.

Right. He *wasn't* going to let it drop.

Finally, she forced herself to say, "Five years ago today…I killed someone."

For a minute he didn't utter a word. He simply cuddled her to him once more. Then he said, ''When you were a police officer.''

She nodded against his chest.

There was a long pause before he said, ''And it still gets to you this badly.''

''Yes,'' she whispered, her throat tight.

''Then...look, I'm sorry I pushed. If it's too hard to talk about, don't.''

A renegade tear trickled down her cheek.

Noah wiped it away, his touch ever so tender. And suddenly it seemed terribly important that she *not* shut him out.

If there was going to be anything between them, anything serious and lasting...

Maybe it was premature, but that was the way she'd begun thinking this silly ''partnership'' of theirs might turn out. Serious and lasting. Perhaps even permanent.

And if she felt like that, shouldn't she be able to tell him about her worst demons?

He wanted to help. So even though she didn't see how he possibly could, shouldn't she give him the chance to try? No matter how hard she found it?

CHAPTER THIRTEEN

DANA TOOK ANOTHER DEEP breath, then sat up straight so she could see Noah's reactions to her words.

"He was just a kid," she reluctantly began. "Only seventeen years old."

"Oh, Dana," Noah murmured, reaching for her hands.

"But I didn't realize he was *that* young until later, because everything happened in fast forward."

She could already see his face in her mind's eye, so she mentally backed up to the beginning before making herself continue.

"It was one of those sweltering afternoons when even New York slows to a crawl. I was in a cruiser, driving up Third Avenue, and…this car went flying past me.

"A Honda Accord. Silver. With black racing stripes and a spoiler bar. The driver weaving in and out of traffic like a maniac.

"I flipped on my lights and siren and took off in pursuit. And…

"It was like a chase scene from a movie. He side-swiped half a dozen vehicles and almost killed a few pedestrians. Then he caromed off a delivery truck and ended up with his hood halfway through a restaurant window.

"By the time I'd stopped and jumped out of the cruiser, he was standing on the sidewalk with a pistol aimed at me.

"I…" Fresh tears escaped and she couldn't go on.

"Take it easy," Noah said. "There's no rush."

When she'd managed to pull herself together, she said, "I remember screaming at people to get down. And crouching beside the cruiser to draw my own gun.

"I was shaking so hard I almost couldn't get it out of the holster. And…

"He was walking toward me, still pointing his pistol.

"I…Noah, I was practically begging him to drop it but he just kept coming. It was as if he were a robot, as if he couldn't hear me.

"Then he got almost to the cruiser and I was sure he was going to fire if I didn't shoot him. So I did. Only…

"I didn't mean to kill him. I was just trying to stop him. To hit him in the arm. But my aim was off and the bullet went straight through his heart. It just…"

Noah reached for her and held her again, murmuring "It's all right."

But it wasn't. She hadn't told him the worst part yet. And she didn't want to, didn't want to say one more word.

She'd come this far, though, so she forced herself to sit back and meet his gaze again.

"You couldn't help it," he said. "If you hadn't shot him he'd have killed you."

"No," she whispered. "No, he wouldn't have. Because after... His gun wasn't real. It looked real, but it was plastic."

"Dana...you didn't know that."

"No. But...he wanted me to kill him. He planned it. It was...the academic term is *victim-precipitated homicide*. On the job they call it *suicide by cop*."

"You mean this happens often enough that it has names?"

"Yes. And there was...when the detectives arrived they found a note in his glove compartment. Addressed to 'the officer who killed me.'

"It said he was sorry he'd had to involve someone else. That he'd tried to commit suicide and couldn't. But he wanted to die, so... And he said I shouldn't blame myself."

"That's right. You shouldn't."

"I know. At least, my *brain* knows. Even the police report didn't blame me. It classified the death as a justifiable homicide.

"Yet of all the things people said, you know the one that really stuck with me?"

She tried to go on but couldn't.

"What was it?" Noah eventually asked.

She swallowed hard, then forced the next part out. "A senior officer told me I'd made an error in judgment. I'd *just* made an error in judgment was exactly how he put it. He was actually trying to make me feel better, only…"

Noah took her hands in his again. "Dana, have you talked to someone about this? A professional, I mean?"

"Yes. I spent tons of time with a department shrink. He tried to help me work my way through it, but I couldn't.

"I mean, I can rationally tell myself that it wasn't my fault. That the boy was intent on ending his life and…"

She shook her head, aware she was rambling but unable to keep her thoughts organized.

The next thing she knew she was saying, "Researchers have studied police shootings. And a lot of civilians killed in them are looking to die."

"Including your guy," Noah said. "Which means that blaming yourself is simply wrong. It's…

"But I guess my saying that doesn't help. I'm sure you've already gone over the logic a million times."

She nodded, although the number had to be closer to a trillion.

"And then there was my father," she said, jumping to yet another track.

Now that she'd gotten started, every single detail seemed to want to pour out.

"He was really proud that I'd followed in his footsteps," she continued. "So when I had to quit…

"He never said anything. I mean, he told me he

understood. But I knew how much I'd disappointed him.''

"Do you think you could have overestimated that?'' Noah said slowly.

"Uh-uh. He's my *father*. I've been reading him my entire life.''

"Even so, nobody can ever be certain how another person feels about something. So maybe you should talk to him. You might discover he really *did* understand.''

"No, I can't. If I raised the subject he'd realize how much it still bothers me. Then he'd worry. I just…it wouldn't be a good idea.''

Noah was silent for a minute before saying, "You said you *had* to quit. Why, when nobody blamed you?''

"*I* blamed me. Regardless of what was rational, I couldn't get past the fact I'd killed that boy. Couldn't make myself stop thinking I should have been able to tell his gun wasn't real. That I shouldn't have made an error in judgment. That I—''

"You *didn't* make an error. You—''

"I *did*, Noah. I killed a teenager brandishing a plastic gun. Killed, not merely wounded. And I was afraid that if I ever found myself in a similar situation…

"You know what I think must have bothered my father the most?''

"What?''

"Exactly what you just asked about. The reason I had to quit.

"You see, he's from the school that says if you fall off a horse you get right back on. But I could barely look at my gun afterward.

"Even if my C.O. had *ordered* me to take target practice there'd have been no way I could. I wasn't sure if I'd *ever* be able to pull a trigger again. Regardless of the circumstances.

"I'm still not. And that makes me…

"It makes me a failure as a cop," she forced herself to say.

"That isn't true, Dana. I'll bet you were a great cop. You—"

"Exactly. *Were*. Past tense.

"Noah, we're five years after the fact and I can still hardly touch my gun without having an anxiety attack.

"I never carry it. I only had it with me today because of those damned notes. Normally I keep it locked up so that…

"But getting back to the point, I couldn't be a cop when I knew I might not be able to use my weapon. That would have put innocent lives, including my own, in jeopardy. So I resigned. End of story."

Noah was silent for a long moment. "But it isn't the end of the story," he said at last. "Not when you still have all this leftover…"

"I have post-traumatic-stress syndrome," she supplied. "That's the official diagnosis. And *anniversary reaction* is the term to explain why I went off the deep end because my father happened to innocently say something that...

"Well, July 23 is never a good day for me—to put it mildly."

"Then you know what we should do?"

"What?"

"Just what we originally intended. Go out. Have dinner. Talk about Four Corners. Or any other subject except what day it is."

She hesitated. She felt far too shaky to go out, but she didn't want to be alone. Not when the option was being with Noah.

"Could we phone for a pizza, instead?" she suggested.

"And stay right here, you mean? Just you and me? Alone together?" He gave her one of his killer smiles.

It made her face hot—and started her thinking that for a woman who rarely blushed she'd been doing a lot of it lately. Then he put an end to her thoughts by kissing her.

Once more, his kiss began warm and slow and lingering, but the moment she responded it became more intimate. Which made her response grow more intimate, as well.

She breathed in his sultry scent and caressed his cheek with her fingers. The male roughness of his four-o'clock shadow started an ache deep inside her.

He kissed the corners of her mouth, the corners of her eyes, then kissed his way down her throat.

His warm breath against the hollow of her collarbone sent such hot desire through her that she positively craved his touch. She wanted to make love with this man. Now.

She didn't want to wait until after her work at Four Corners was done, and she suspected that every fiber of her being was sending him that message.

"Hey," he whispered against her skin.

"Hey, what?" she whispered back.

When he shifted position a little, and gazed at her, she could see her own emotions mirrored in the dark depth of his eyes.

Longing. Desire. Need.

"If I could just keep on kissing you all night long, I would," he murmured. "But my self-control won't make it through another thirty seconds.

"And..." He paused, giving her a weary smile. "Hell, I didn't realize I had even *this* much self-control. But after the day you've had, you've got to be so emotionally strung out that...

"What I'm trying to say is I don't want us to do anything you'll regret."

She continued looking at him, drinking him in, unable to stop. But aware he was making sense.

And she should be very, very glad that *one* of them was thinking rationally.

Yet she wanted him very, very badly.

"You know," he said at last. "You feel so good, and smell so good, and taste...I think I deserve a major award for self-denial."

"Would you settle for that pizza?" she made herself say.

NOAH FOLLOWED DANA FROM the kitchen to the living room, his gaze positively glued to the enticing sway of her hips.

After they'd decided to order in, she'd changed out of her "day" clothes. And jeans and a T-shirt accentuated her curves far more than her dress had done. So much more that the way she looked—or maybe he should say the way he was reacting to it—had him seriously thinking he'd better head home.

But he didn't want to. Not even a little.

It would still be July 23 for a few more hours. And although she seemed back to her usual self, leaving her on her own might not be a good idea. Yet if he stayed…

Regardless of how she *seemed* to be, he'd bet she was still feeling fragile as hell. Which meant that tonight would be a really bad time to add any more emotional complications to the mix.

So if he stayed he'd have to keep his distance. Because every time he got too close he couldn't help touching her. And every time he touched her he had one hell of a time stopping.

That in mind, instead of sitting down with her, he wandered over to the window and stood looking out into the lingering light—wondering how it was possible that almost no time ago he'd never even heard of Ms. Dana Morancy.

Man, oh man. If anyone had ever told him he'd be falling in love with a woman he'd barely met he'd have said they were crazy. But that was exactly what was happening.

What else would explain why he couldn't take his eyes off her? And why, when they weren't together, he spent ninety-nine percent of his time thinking about her? Or why just looking at her made him want to hold her in his arms?

"Noah?"

He turned toward her. Sure enough, that was all it took. He was dying to hold her again.

"We never did get around to talking about Four Corners," she said. "Do you want to do some brainstorming now?"

"Why not."

Casually, he crossed the room and sat down on the far end of the couch from her.

She gave him a wan smile that strongly tempted him to move closer. He managed to resist.

"Aside from Chris Vidal," she said, "is there anyone you've been thinking could be our guy?"

Now what did he do?

He thought rapidly. She'd promised Larry that she'd talk to Paul Coulter tomorrow. And hopefully Tony Zicco, as well. That would keep her busy for a good part of the day *and* keep her away from head office.

So maybe it made sense to leave telling her who his other prime suspect was for a bit longer. Because once he *did* tell her there'd be no turning back. And if he was wrong...

The apartment's buzzer sounded, giving him a temporary reprieve from having to decide.

"Your father again?" he asked as she rose.

"I doubt it, but I'm beyond predicting."

He watched her walk over to the hall and press the intercom button, saying, "Yes?"

"Got a package for Dana Morancy," a man said.

"From where?" she asked, glancing back into the living room with a puzzled expression.

"Lady, I'm a cabbie. I got paid to deliver it. That's all I know."

"Okay, I'll be right down.

"You don't have to come," she added as Noah pushed himself up.

"I wouldn't mind stretching my legs."

He followed her along the hall and down the stairs, to where an impatient-looking man was waiting at the front door, holding a cardboard box tied with string. A taxi stood on the street behind him.

Noah fished in his pocket for a tip while Dana took the box. A quick look told him there were no markings on it except for her name and address.

"A bomb, you figure?" he asked as she closed the door.

"Very funny," she said, but she did hold the box up to her ear for a few seconds as they headed for the stairs.

Back in her apartment, she set it on the kitchen

table, took a pair of scissors from a drawer and cut the string.

"Careful," he said as she started to lift the lid.

"Noah! Don't try to make me nervous."

"I'm not. But we don't know what's in there."

"Well, we're going to find out."

She slid the lid off and set it to one side.

He peered over her shoulder as she folded back the tissue paper... And realized what was inside at the same instant she murmured, "Oh, Lord."

"Don't touch it," he ordered. "Not until we've had a closer look."

Gingerly, he tipped the box until the little rag doll slid out onto the table. Then they just stood staring at it.

It had a couple of long hat pins stuck into its chest—some joker's idea of a voodoo doll. Which wouldn't have been half as disconcerting if it wasn't supposed to represent Dana.

But it was. A cutout photograph of her face was taped over the doll's.

"Okay," she whispered. "Okay, that's the picture from my Dana Mayfield Web site."

Right. The one he'd sat gazing at on his screen last week.

Dana picked up the doll, removed the hat pins and set them aside, then thoroughly examined it.

"There's nothing unusual," she finally said, her voice sounding marginally more normal. "Nothing except for the picture. And virtually anyone could have printed it off. But who did?''

She looked at Noah, nervously licking her lips.

He almost didn't want to ask, but he said, ''Is there a note?''

''Oh, Lord,'' she murmured again.

He took the tissue out of the box, revealing a white envelope. A pair of disposable latex gloves were neatly folded around it.

''The *no prints* message again?'' he said, without touching anything.

''Uh-huh.''

When Dana didn't reach for the envelope, he did. The note inside read:

What is wrong with you? Don't you value your life? Stay away from Four Corners.

Dolly's your final warning. Remember, I know where you live.

His stomach had begun churning. He hated to imagine what Dana's must be doing.

''I should check this print against the other notes,'' she said.

''It's going to be the same.''

''Probably. But I should make sure.''

Still clutching the doll, she took the note from him and turned toward the kitchen doorway.

He trailed after her to the front hall, where she'd left her briefcase, then over to the couch.

Silently, he waited while she put the doll on the coffee table and took her gun out of the case. After setting it beside the doll, she dug out the other two notes and compared them with the new one.

"They all match, don't they," he said at last.

"Yes. All run off on *my* printer."

Her glance flickered to him and back to the notes as she added, "That means someone was in my office again, even though the lock's been fixed."

Someone who knew where she lived. He *really* didn't like that part.

"Dana, this time, you *have* to call the police."

"No. If I did that the job at Four Corners would be totally blown. And my professional reputation right along with it."

Ordering himself to stay as calm as he could, he said, "You told me you discussed the case with your father."

When she nodded, he added, "Did you tell him about the notes?"

"No."

"Because, if you did, *he'd* want you to call the cops, right?"

"Yes, but only because I'm his daughter. If I were some other P.I. he'd accept that I really can't."

"Look," he said, sitting down next to her, "no job's worth risking your life for."

She slowly shook her head. "There isn't much risk. I mean, I doubt my life's really in danger. As I said before, these notes are likely just a scare tactic."

"And if they aren't?"

"If they aren't... Well, as I *also* said before, I have my gun."

"Which you're not sure you could use."

She didn't reply to that. Instead, she took the notes and the doll over to the desk that stood in front of the window and tucked them away in it.

"Out of sight, out of mind?" he said when she turned back toward him.

"Noah...killers don't issue warnings. If whoever's doing this really meant what he said I'd already be lying in the morgue.

"The second note told me I'd be dead sorry if I ever came back to Four Corners, remember? But I did and I'm still alive."

"Dana, I just want you to stay that way."

"I will. Don't worry."

Don't worry? The woman he loved was getting death threats and expected him not to worry?

The instant that thought formed he realized his brain had notched the ante up from "falling in love with" to simply "in love with."

He didn't know how that could possibly have happened so quickly, but he had no time to think about it at the moment.

Right now, he had to focus on ensuring Dana *did* stay alive.

"I've never used a gun," he said. "Show me how."

SIMPLY HOLDING HER GUN might have Dana shaking inside, but she intended to keep that to herself. She'd shared enough with Noah already.

Aside from the department shrink, she'd told him more about the shooting—and the emotional aftermath—than she'd told another living soul. And she wasn't entirely sure how she felt about the fact that she'd come to trust him with her innermost secrets.

Forcing that thought away and getting back to the task at hand, she said to him, "Okay, this is a SIG Sauer P226, 9 mm. It's lighter than a lot of automatics, so it's easier to use. And this is how you put the clip in."

She demonstrated removing and shoving it in again, then passed him the gun—aware of the tiny rush of relief she felt at merely getting it out of her hand.

"That lever on the left side is the safety," she continued. "You push it down if you're going to be shooting, but never touch it otherwise. Give it a try."

She watched him move the lever down and back up, then said, "Fine. Now, take out the clip and I'll show you a proper stance."

Once he'd set the clip on the coffee table, she told him to hold the SIG with both hands and point it at her desk. Then she stepped behind him and wrapped her arms around him to check his grip.

Even as she was doing so, she knew she was in trouble.

The maleness of his scent started interfering with

her brain, and the moment her breasts pressed against his back her nipples hardened. If she had an internal alarm system, its siren would have begun screaming.

Trying her best to ignore the sensation of his body heat seeping through her, she shifted her pelvis so their lower bodies were in alignment—which proved a major mistake.

Hot desire jolted through her, making her mouth go dry and her pulse begin a crazy dance.

Exhaling slowly, she repositioned his fingers a little, and said, "Okay, that feels right."

"It sure does," he murmured.

She licked her lips, then took a backward step, breaking their contact.

"Not anymore," he said, glancing around at her.

"Noah…"

"Just joking." He looked toward the desk again.

Assuring herself she was fine now that she wasn't touching him, she said, "Okay. Push the safety off and fire."

A moment later, the gun made a clicking noise.

"Good," she said, moving a little farther back. "That's basically what you do.

"But a loaded gun jumps when you pull the trigger, so you have to aim lower than you think you should. Your shots will go higher than you're expecting."

"Got it."

Turning toward her once more, he put the SIG down, saying, "This is all well and good, but I *still* think you should call the cops."

"No. I'm going to see things through on my own. See them through with you, I should say."

"Yeah. With me. But has anyone ever mentioned that you're one of the most stubborn people on earth?"

"Well…there was my mother. My father. My C.O. on the job. Should I continue?"

Noah shook his head, his thoughts returning to where they'd been before that damned doll had arrived.

Did he tell her now or wait a while longer?

She could say the notes were likely just scare tactics. Say she doubted her life was actually in danger. But saying didn't make something so. And if anything happened to her…

He couldn't even bear to think about that, which told him he didn't really have any choice.

"Let's sit down," he made himself say. "There's something I'd better not put off telling you any longer."

CHAPTER FOURTEEN

IT WAS OBVIOUS TO DANA that Noah was highly reluctant to start in on whatever he was about to say.

Her clue was the amount of time he spent talking
to Doc, who was trying to decide whether or not he'd
rather sit on the couch with them or head back to the
bedroom.

When the cat finally made his decision and disap-
peared, she could almost see Noah mentally gearing
up.

At last, he said, "Earlier, you asked if I suspected
anyone besides Chris."

"Uh-huh?"

"Well, I do."

She nodded for him to continue, glad to hear he
had another possibility in mind. Because while she
hadn't entirely eliminated Chris Vidal, she doubted
he was the one.

There was a long pause before Noah said, "Larry."

"Larry Benzer?"

Even as she spoke she realized it was a dumb question. What *other* Larry would he be referring to?

"Right," he said. "That's the real reason I was

doing my sleuthing on the quiet. The real reason I didn't say anything about it to the bosses.

"If it *is* Larry, I've been playing with dynamite. And even if it isn't, if he ever got wind that I'd thought it might be him…"

"You could kiss your job goodbye," she concluded. "Whether Robert's your uncle or not."

"Exactly."

As quickly as she could, she thought back through her brief interactions with Larry.

Right from the beginning she'd had the feeling he didn't really want her at Four Corners. And he'd made her a bit uneasy. Then, this afternoon, when he'd been so dogmatic…

She focused on Noah once more. "I'm thinking about Larry wanting me to search the warehouse."

"Yeah, I've been thinking about that ever since you mentioned it. He's been trying so hard to convince us that the saboteur just has to be one of those guys, I can't help wondering if he's planning to plant some fake evidence—pointing straight at one of them."

"Great minds," she said. "He'd plant something, I'd find it, and bingo. Case closed."

"It might make more sense to search Larry's office," Noah said.

She wasn't sure he was serious, but his next words showed he clearly was.

"If we're guessing right, then you might find the

evidence there. Before he gets around to planting it in the warehouse.''

She considered the idea. It definitely had merit, although she wasn't comfortable with some of the ramifications.

''Let's give that more thought later,'' she said. ''At the moment we should get down to facts. What makes you suspect him?''

''He needs money.''

''Really.'' *Very* interesting. ''How do you know that?''

''He told me. Not long before the problems started he said he needed a couple of hundred thou' and asked me to arrange taking it out of the company for him.''

''Really,'' she said again. Serious money. More interesting by the minute.

''He assumed I could do it easily,'' Noah continued. ''Because back when Four Corners was privately held, whenever there was a lot of money sitting in the bank he and Robert would pay themselves a healthy dividend.

''But he hadn't realized how completely the rules changed when they went public. Now, if the board declares a dividend it has to be paid out to thousands of shareholders.

''And there's absolutely no way we could pay a big enough one to let Larry end up with as much as he was after. Even though he holds a lot of shares, we couldn't come anywhere close.''

Dana nodded, trying not to let herself grow convinced that Larry was their man until she had far more details.

"If he owns a lot of shares," she said, "why wouldn't he have just sold some of them? After you told him you couldn't go the dividend route, I mean."

"He can't sell *any*. Neither can Robert. Not until Four Corners has been publicly traded for five years. That was a clause in the IPO."

Her brain took a second to translate that into initial public offering. Once it had, she said, "Is that sort of restriction usual?"

"Well, five years is longer than normal, but the clause itself isn't uncommon. By agreeing to it, the principals are indicating they have faith in the company's future."

She nodded again, then asked, "Did Larry tell you why he needed so *much* money?"

"Uh-huh. The story was that Martha wants to renovate their apartment. Plus, their two eldest kids are in college and the third one's due to start next year, so he's got major expenses on that front."

"And exactly what did he say when you explained that a dividend was out of the question?"

"He asked if there was some other way of getting money from the company."

"And...?"

"I said the only possibility for it was to give him a loan. But that would require the board's approval.

And since the board's no longer basically just him and Robert, the idea would never fly.''

"Why not?"

"It's the sort of thing minority shareholders get really upset about. They figure there are better uses for a company's funds than making loans to its executives.''

That made sense, even to someone like her who was no expert on the intricacies of how public companies were run.

"And it was after he learned there was no way of getting his money from Four Corners," she said thoughtfully, "that the problems started.''

"Right. The problems started and the share price began to sink. Of course, the timing could have been mere coincidence. His needing money doesn't necessarily mean he's the one behind the plot.''

"It well might, though.''

And it was such a *simple* plot. She'd thought that way back at the start, when Robert had first mentioned it. All the saboteur needed was an accomplice to buy up shares on the cheap, then sell them when the price rose again.

"Assuming it *is* Larry," she said, "who do you think he's got accumulating shares?''

Noah shook his head. "He knows a lot of people. He'd have approached someone he was sure he could trust. Someone who had no problem with the idea of making money illegally.

"And we can add 'risk taker' to the profile. If the

Securities Exchange Commission people ever got wind of what was going on, *both* Larry and his friend would end up in jail.''

''It would also have to be someone with a pile of money,'' she said.

When Noah didn't look as if he was so sure about that, she added, ''If Larry needs money, then he obviously doesn't have a bunch of it sitting in the bank. And *someone* has to have the money to buy those shares. I mean, even if the price is depressed they're not free.''

''That's true, but a lot of people who are in the market have margin accounts—which means they can basically play with borrowed money. Or we could be talking an investment line of credit from a bank.''

''Right, I wasn't thinking along those lines.''

''But it all adds up pretty neatly, doesn't it,'' Noah said, shaking his head. ''I just wish I'd managed to find some real proof.''

She wished he had, too. Because even though it all *did* seem to add up neatly, something struck her as wrong with the picture.

Why wouldn't a man like Larry, who'd been making a lot of money for a lot of years, have built up adequate college funds for his children?

And surely he couldn't figure it was worth risking a jail term to renovate his apartment. No matter how much Martha wanted to do it.

''There's another thing,'' Noah said.

''What?''

"After the problems started, when Robert and I came up with the stock manipulation theory, Larry initially dismissed it. Which at the time I thought was very strange, because it seemed so obvious that we could be onto something."

"But if he was the one behind the manipulating, he'd naturally try to convince you that it *wasn't* a likely scenario."

"Exactly." Noah eyed her for a few seconds, then said, "So where do we go from here?"

"I'm not sure," she said slowly. "I've never been involved in anything like this before—a situation where someone who hired me turns into a viable suspect. I don't quite know how to handle it."

"Robert hired you," Noah pointed out. "Not Larry."

"Well...that isn't quite true. Robert's the one I initially met with, the one who officially offered me the job. And maybe the only one who actually *wanted* to hire a P.I.

"But I'm not working for him, personally. I mean, he isn't paying me out of his own pocket."

"Yeah, you're right. My brain must have gone onto pause. Since Four Corners is paying your invoices, you're working for both of them."

She nodded. "And that gives me a lot of pause when it comes to the idea of searching Larry's office.

"I think...I think I'd have to discuss it with Robert, first."

"You mean tell him you suspect Larry?"

"Yes."

"He'd ask why."

"I know. And I'd need to give him an explanation that didn't involve you. But I'll think of something. I...let me sleep on it."

Noah hesitated, then said, "Is that my cue to go?"

She should say yes. Yet she so, so badly didn't want him to leave.

When she said nothing, he looked at the desk—where she'd stashed the voodoo doll and the notes.

"Would Larry do that sort of thing?" she asked, her gaze following his. "Try to frighten me off with scare tactics?"

He shook his head. "At this point I'm not sure what anyone would do. But...I assume you have a shoulder holster for your gun?"

"Yes, of course."

"Then...I understand how hard it would be, but do you think you could start wearing it? Until we get this sorted out? Because even if you keep on carrying it in your briefcase, it's not exactly..."

"I don't know whether I could or not," she murmured, just the thought enough to unsettle her stomach.

"I really wish you'd try. And..." He glanced toward the desk again, then back at her. "Dana, whoever it is, that line about knowing where you live... After I leave, I'm going to spend the rest of the night worrying."

As would she, she silently admitted.

Once he was gone, she wouldn't go to bed. She'd sit here trying not to think frightening thoughts and pretend she didn't hear strange noises.

She'd gotten very little sleep last night. And it had been a long, emotionally draining day.

But even though she desperately needed a good eight hours, if she let herself fall asleep she'd have nightmares.

Reruns of last night's. Maybe even new, worse ones.

"So...what if I stay and sleep on your couch?" Noah suggested. "Nothing else. Just sleep here with your gun beside me."

"Like a bodyguard."

"Yeah, I guess."

She almost smiled at the irony.

A bodyguard who'd never used a gun. Looking out for a licensed investigator who didn't know if she could ever use one again.

"What do you think?" he said.

She was tempted to tell him the truth. To say she'd rather have him in her bed than on her couch. Instead, she said, "You don't figure you'd be too uncomfortable?"

DANA PAID THE CABBIE who'd brought her back from Tony Zicco's apartment in Brooklyn, then climbed out into the steamy afternoon and crossed the street to Four Corners—hoping against hope that she'd find Noah standing in the reception area.

He was nowhere in sight, and when she glanced down the hallway toward his office its door was closed.

Since "circumspect" precluded marching down and banging on it with the receptionist watching, she swallowed her disappointment and headed for the stairs, telling herself she did *not* need to see him right this minute.

It wasn't as if she hadn't heard from him today. He'd called twice on her cell, to check in and make sure she was okay. But she hadn't actually *seen* him. And ridiculous as it was, that made the day seem ten years long.

When she'd woken this morning he'd already left, although she'd gathered from his note that she'd missed him by mere minutes.

He'd gone home to shower and change, the note had said, because he had an early meeting uptown.

"Catch you later, Noah," he'd ended it. Then he'd added, "And *please* think about wearing your gun."

She *had* thought about it. But she'd ultimately taken only a couple of baby steps in that direction.

She'd put the SIG into its holster before stashing it in her briefcase. And she'd brought along a loose-fitting linen jacket with bat-wing sleeves that would be perfect for concealment.

However, when she'd gone to the warehouse to talk with Paul Coulter she'd left the gun behind. She'd done the same when she'd made the trip to see Tony after lunch—both times telling herself it was simply too hot for even a light jacket, and that the chance of being in any danger was awfully remote.

And it had been. Now that she'd spent a good amount of time with all three of the warehouse workers, the possibility that one of them was the saboteur seemed even less likely than it had before.

Oh, she hadn't forgotten that Chris Vidal had told her Tony wasn't totally reliable. But that was true of a lot of people. And neither Tony nor Paul had said anything to raise a single new doubt in her mind.

She reached the top of the stairs and gave Helen Rupert a quick wave before starting down the hall to her office. When she got to the door she paused, remembering that the other morning Noah had been waiting inside for her.

Not this time, though, and she felt a fresh pang of disappointment at seeing he wasn't there. But that was just silly.

She shut the door, sank into her chair and sat rubbing her bare arms, thinking air-conditioning was a mixed blessing. After the heat outside, the building felt like an igloo.

Then her gaze drifted to the phone and she spent the next minute or two staring at it, willing Noah to call. That didn't produce results, but just as she was about to give up her cellular rang.

When she answered it her father said, "Where are you?"

"Well, hi to you, too," she teased. "I'm at Four Corners. Why?"

"Oh, nothing, except I figured you might be lying dead someplace. You promised to call me last night, remember? After you got back from dinner with Noah Haine? Discuss the thoughts I have about your case?"

Oh, Lord, she'd completely forgotten.

"Dad, I'm sorry. I guess I've got too much on my mind. But I definitely want to hear your ideas."

"Then how about dinner tonight?"

She thought rapidly. Unless Robert objected, she'd be searching Larry's office tonight.

"Or are you having dinner with *Noah* again?" her father pressed.

His tone warned her that he was hoping he wouldn't even hear a "maybe" in reply, so she said, "No, but I'm just not sure tonight will work for me. Can I let you know later?"

"Later I'll have gone home."

"Then, if I can, I'll come to the house, okay? We can eat in the neighborhood. Or order in. I'll call and let you know, all right?"

"Sure," he said.

He still didn't sound pleased. And she had the distinct impression that he'd taken a serious dislike to Noah—which was the *last* thing she wanted.

But she didn't have either the time or the energy to worry about that right now, and once she'd said goodbye her thoughts immediately focused on the issue of Larry.

How on earth was she going to handle that with Robert?

There wasn't much time left before their four-thirty appointment, and she still hadn't come up with a way of explaining how she knew Larry needed money. Not without implicating Noah.

If she couldn't manage to do that, then she wouldn't be able to use the money angle, which would make her case for suspecting Larry far weaker. But all she had to do was convince Robert...

Maybe a "better safe than sorry" approach would work.

Deciding that was what she'd have to go with, she rubbed her arms again. They felt so cold that she pushed back her chair and retrieved her jacket from the coat tree in the corner.

As she shrugged into it, she noticed there was something in one of its big pockets. Absently, she stuck her hand in to see what it was—and when she felt stuffed fabric and paper her heart stopped.

Almost certain she knew what she'd found, she pulled it out.

Sure enough, it was the head of a rag doll. With her face taped on it and stuffing sticking out of the bottom of its neck.

Her heart started racing now, and she dropped the head as if it had just exploded into flames.

The jacket had been hanging in her office since she'd arrived this morning. So sometime between then and now their guy had been in here. Yet again.

The hairs on her arms suddenly stood on end as something else occurred to her. If this was the head from the doll he'd had delivered to her last night, then he'd been in her apartment as well.

That was a possibility she didn't want to even consider.

She couldn't stand to think about some lunatic wandering around her place. Handling her things. Poking around in her desk and anywhere else he wanted to.

Merely imagining it creeped her out.

And what about Doc? He'd have been terrified if a stranger had come in. And what if...

No. Nobody would have harmed Doc. He'd have hidden. An intruder wouldn't even have known she had a cat.

Unless he'd noticed the kitty litter, which wouldn't exactly be hard to do.

She made a conscious effort to relax her shoulder muscles and told herself she was undoubtedly worrying for nothing. This head had to be from a different doll.

Definitely.

No doubt about it.

But regardless of that, she just knew her weirdo had left another note with it.

Her heart still beating fast, she reached into her pocket again—and retrieved an envelope from the bottom. A small one this time. Pocket-size.

Nervously licking her lips, she removed the note and read:

Three strikes, you're out. Three warnings, too.

Now you're into sudden-death overtime. Start saying your prayers.

The words made her half frightened, half angry.

She was tired of this game. Fed up with what she was almost—but not entirely—certain were empty threats. So damned ticked off that she walked back to her desk, slid her jacket off and did something she hadn't been able to force herself to do in five years.

She removed the holstered SIG from her briefcase and put it on.

Then she slipped into her jacket again and took a long, slow breath.

Her stomach felt queasy and her chest was tight, but she'd done it. She was wearing her gun and she was going to keep it on for the time being. And if it turned out those threats *weren't* empty…

Well, she thought she could go as far as drawing her gun. Although anything more…

Telling herself not to even think about that, she forced her mind back to the latest note. There was something wrong with it, and her brain finally clicked on to what.

Her father was a sports fan, so she'd grown up going to Yankees games. ''Three strikes, you're out'' was a familiar phrase. However, baseball didn't have sudden-death overtime. It had extra innings. Overtime was hockey.

Mixed references. Did that mean their guy was sports illiterate?

She pulled the desk phone closer and dialed Noah's office extension.

"Noah Haine," he said, picking up.

"It's me."

"Hey, are you back?"

"Yes."

"Good. How did it go with Tony? And how is he?"

"Fine to both. But I have to ask you something. Is Larry into sports?"

"Yeah, why?"

"Baseball?"

"The biggest Mets fan in the city. Why?"

"Noah, there's another note."

A second of silence, during which she refrained from adding, *and a severed head.*

Then he said, "I'll be right up."

CHAPTER FIFTEEN

NOAH READ THE NOTE, then set it on the desk, next to the doll's head he'd picked up off the floor. He desperately wanting to *insist* that the time had come to call the cops, but by now he knew Dana well enough to realize that she'd only dig her heels in again. So what was the point?

"Noah?" she said quietly.

When he looked at her, she drew back the left side of her jacket. Revealing her gun.

Seeing it made him feel immensely better—both about her safety and her state of mind.

"Hey," he said. "You did it. Congratulations. That's a giant step."

"It's a scary step," she told him. "I feel as if I'm in the midst of a never-ending panic attack."

"I bet that'll gradually fade. And you'll forget you even have it on."

He stepped closer, wrapped his arms around her and held her tight—wondering how he'd lived for so many years without realizing just how soft and warm and sexy a woman could feel against him.

The right woman. The woman who, if anything awful happened to her…

As he was telling himself not to think about that, she said, "I can't stop wondering if it's Larry. Do *you* figure he did this? That he's done everything?"

Reluctantly, Noah took a backward step so he could see her face. "You're *certain* you locked your office?"

"I can't believe you'd even ask. Of course I did."

"Then it had to be *someone* with a master."

"Not necessarily. It could have been someone with a talent for picking locks. That would take longer, so there'd be more risk of being seen, but it isn't out of the question."

He wearily shook his head, wishing they had more facts and fewer unknowns.

"What about the three strikes, sudden death?" she said. "You think there's any significance to that?"

"I don't know. Maybe he simply didn't consider— or didn't care—that it's different sports. Maybe he just thought it sounded good."

"You really are sure it's Larry, aren't you?"

"Yeah. Pretty much."

He drew her near once more, adding, "Listen, I was almost on my way out when you phoned. I have to see our bank manager about a few things. So call me on my cell as soon as you're finished with Robert, okay? Let me know what's happening?"

As she murmured "Sure" against his chest, he lightly kissed the top of her head.

Her hair smelled like a country meadow, and she

felt so good in his arms that he wanted her to stay right where she was for…for the rest of their lives.

The words weren't much more than a sigh in his mind, but he knew they were true. He wanted to be with Dana Morancy till the end of time. And he didn't want the end of time to come too soon.

He kissed her again, then his gaze shifted to her desk. To the doll's head. To the note.

Sudden-death overtime, it read. *Death.*

He couldn't help thinking that Larry was a Vietnam vet. Which meant there was absolutely no doubt he knew how to use a gun.

"COME IN," ROBERT SAID, giving Dana a warm smile as she arrived for their meeting.

She smiled back, hoping she didn't seem nervous but almost sure she did. She was still feeling very, very uncomfortable about wearing her gun. And when she added that to the prospect of…

Well, she was definitely *not* looking forward to telling Robert that his partner of thirty years had become her front runner in the saboteur race.

He'd hardly be pleased to hear it, and if he figured there was no way Larry could be guilty she might well find herself out on her ear.

When she sat down across from him, he said, "Helen mentioned that you went to see Tony Zicco. How is he?"

"A little dozy from painkillers, but aside from that he seemed pretty good."

"He wasn't too dozy to talk about the problems at the warehouse?"

"No. He wasn't reluctant to, either. Both Stu and Paul had told me he felt terrible about messing up on the container delivery, and they weren't exaggerating. He went on and on about it—as if I were a priest in a confessional."

"So you don't think…"

She shook her head. "Unless I uncover something new and startling down the line, I really can't see that it's any of the warehouse people."

"You're sure? Even though you had the feeling Stu was lying? That he didn't really rush off that day to meet his wife?"

"Well, I still don't think he did, but I don't think he was intentionally avoiding that ship's arrival, either."

She paused, then made herself say, "Robert, there's something very awkward I have to raise."

"Oh?"

"I…there isn't an easy way of saying this, but I think it's conceivable—and I'm only talking a possibility—that Larry's behind the sabotage."

She waited while Robert sat back in his chair, his expression unreadable.

"Why?" he said at last. "What makes you think it could be him?"

"Nothing concrete. Just several things that, combined, make me wonder."

"What things?"

"Well, for one, that he's so intent on trying to convince us it *has* to be someone from the warehouse."

"The 'he doth protest too much' school of thought."

"Exactly," she said, feeling a little more at ease now that she saw Robert was going to listen, that he wasn't leaping blindly to Larry's defense.

"What else?" he said.

"He has a master key. He'd have no difficulty getting in and out of the warehouse."

"The arson and the crates," Robert said.

"Uh-huh. Plus, he was talking to me yesterday and mentioned that he knows the security guard's routine."

"Anything more?"

She nodded, reminding herself she was walking a tightrope when it came to what she said.

Noah had discussed a lot of things with her that he'd have never talked about to a real OD consultant. And Robert had no idea that Noah had seen through her cover.

So even though she already knew the answer, she asked, "Was it you who came up with the stock-manipulation theory?"

"Yes. Noah and I."

"Well, you know, right from the start that struck me as a highly probably explanation. Yet Larry seems to…almost pooh-pooh it."

"Yes, he does," Robert slowly agreed. "He's far more convinced that someone's simply out to get us.

Or so he says. But go on. There's still more that bothers you, isn't there?''

She nodded again, dearly wishing she could tell him she knew that Larry had been trying to come up with a lot of money.

However, since she still hadn't figured out how she could do that without involving Noah, she said, ''When Larry and I were talking yesterday, he suggested I search the warehouse after hours. In fact, he pretty well insisted on it.''

For the first time, Robert's expression revealed surprise.

''What does he think you'd find?''

''He said maybe a clue that someone there is guilty. Or maybe even proof. And I can't stop wondering…if he *is* the one…I think he might have decided to plant something for me to find.''

''Ah. And I assume you're thinking you should go along with his suggestion? See if you *do* find anything?''

''Well…what I'm really thinking is that I'd like to have a look around Larry's office. Tonight. See if I turn up anything *there*.''

''Ah,'' Robert said a second time.

''But I didn't want to do it without getting your okay.''

''I'm glad of that. And of course, you couldn't do it without someone letting you into the building. And into his office.''

''Yes. Of course. Only…''

Only Noah could let her in. And she knew there was no way in the world that he wouldn't insist on being right there with her. So she couldn't have Robert around, as well.

"In case Larry *isn't* the one," she said, "and... well, if anything about this ever came to light, from your perspective it would be better if you'd had no apparent involvement. If Larry never knew you'd approved it, I mean.

"So rather than letting me in, I think it would be better to just lend me your master key. If you're okay with my having a look."

Robert stared silently at the floor for several seconds, then met her gaze again. "Yes, I'm okay with it. Mostly because I've been suspicious of Larry myself."

"Really." She hadn't expected that.

"I don't *want* to believe he could be behind things, and I hope to hell he isn't, but there's something you don't know. He's pressed for money."

"Really," she said again.

"Uh-huh. Apparently his kids' college bills are astronomical. And he's looking at some other expenses, as well.

"But the point is, a few months ago he suggested we take a significant amount of cash out of the company.

"It's something we'd done before, and I told him it was fine with me. But when he asked Noah to arrange it, he discovered we can't do it any longer.

"Because of being a public company now and all," Robert added, gesturing with his hand as if that would make the explanation clear.

"At any rate, he told me Noah had said it wasn't doable and that was the last I heard. I thought he'd say something later about having gotten a bank loan or whatever. He didn't, though.

"So in the back of my mind I've had this nagging question. But, as I said, I really don't want to believe it might be him, which I guess is why I kept quiet about it."

"I understand."

Robert gave her a weary shrug. "I should have told you right at the start."

"That's okay. You've told me now. So...what about tonight?"

He wordlessly stared at the floor again. Then, at last, he reached into his pocket and produced his keys.

"And you'll need the code to deactivate the alarm system," he said, jotting down the numbers.

BACK IN HER OWN OFFICE, Dana called and left a message on her father's machine—telling him she was sorry but she wouldn't be able to have dinner with him tonight, after all.

"Let's try to make it tomorrow, for sure," she guiltily added before saying goodbye. Then she clicked off and dialed Noah's cellular number.

When he answered, she simply said, "It's a go."

"I'll meet you at your place," he told her.

Quickly, she changed into her sneakers and headed out. It was well after five, so odds were that Larry had already left. But if he hadn't she didn't want him trapping her again.

She felt less uneasy once she was out of the building, but the closer to home she got the more anxious she grew.

Despite having assured herself a million times that the chopped-off doll's head wasn't from the doll she'd left lying in her apartment this morning, she knew, deep down, that it might be. And if it was...

What if her place had been trashed? And what if Doc was...

No. Doc was just fine.

For the final couple of blocks she silently repeated that like a mantra. Then, as she neared her building, she could see Noah waiting outside for her.

It made her realize just how much she didn't want to go in alone. And now she didn't have to.

When he spotted her he strode down the street toward her—then pulled her into his arms and gave her a lingering kiss.

"That wasn't circumspect," she teased as he let her go.

"To hell with circumspect."

He draped an arm around her waist and they walked along to her front door.

"How soon do we get started?" he asked as she slid her key into the lock.

Miraculously, it worked without her having to coax
if five times.

After telling herself that was a good omen, she said,
"It depends. Does Larry ever come back to the office
after he's left? Ever work there in the evenings?"

"Not that I know of."

"Then there's no point in waiting. I think only
Robert was still in the building when I left. So if you
call his office while I change, and make sure he's
gone…"

They started up the stairs, her pulse beating fast.

"What's wrong?" Noah asked.

She glanced at him, thinking he'd learned to read
her awfully well.

"Nothing, really," she said. "Just…that stupid
doll's head. Even though I know it's not from the doll
I left here…"

"Give me your keys."

She hesitated a moment then did so. Even though
letting him go in first was chicken of her. Especially
when she was the one wearing a gun.

On the other hand, maybe that wasn't significant—
considering they both knew she'd probably never be
able to make herself use it.

They headed down the third-floor hallway and she
held her breath while he unlocked her door.

Then she let herself breathe again when he stepped
inside and said, "Everything looks okay."

As she followed him in, he walked across the living

room to her desk and checked the drawer she'd stashed the doll and notes in.

"Still here," he told her. "Complete with head."

"Thank heavens," she said.

When Doc appeared, cautiously because he'd heard Noah's voice, she picked him up and gave him a good cuddle.

"Hey," Noah said softly, "I'd never have believed I'd be jealous of a cat."

She looked at him. There was so much warmth in his dark gaze that she had to smile.

If she could freeze the instant and keep it forever, she would. Because right this moment everything seemed wonderful in her little corner of the world.

NOAH GLANCED ACROSS the car at Dana as they neared Four Corners.

He was still wearing his suit, but she'd changed into a pair of creamy cotton pants and a loose-fitting shirt the color of her eyes. Raw silk, he thought the fabric was called. Classy, whatever it was.

But she always looked classy. And right now she seemed as calm and collected as if they were merely going out for a drink, rather than on a reconnaissance mission.

He, in sharp contrast, was neither calm nor collected. His adrenaline had started pumping even before they'd left her apartment. Which didn't really make a whole lot of sense, considering that searching an office in an empty building had to involve zero risk.

Or did it?

If that was the case, Dana would have left her gun at home, wouldn't she? And she hadn't.

Even though he knew she still wasn't feeling anywhere near comfortable with it, he'd seen her tuck it into her purse before they'd left her apartment.

"Should I park where I usually do?" he said.

She nodded. "I'll wait in the car until you've made absolutely sure there's nobody inside. Then we'll do our thing."

"Right," he said, although he was far from sure their "thing" would actually get them anywhere.

And that didn't really make a whole lot of sense, either. Not when searching Larry's office had been *his* suggestion.

But the more he'd thought about it, the more he'd wondered how they could hope to find something incriminating when they really had no idea what they were looking for.

At least, he had no idea. And when he'd raised that with Dana she'd just told him that, hopefully, there'd be *something*. And hopefully, they'd know it when they saw it.

That certainly wasn't a scientific approach, but she was the expert so he'd just have to trust her.

Besides, he was really only along for the ride. And to make sure she got in and out with no problems.

He turned into the alley and pulled the Lexus up

behind Four Corners. Then he cut the ignition and resisted the temptation to kiss her for luck.

Experience had taught him that stopping after kissing her once was extremely difficult. Which meant it made sense to get going with what they were here for and leave the kissing until later.

With all kinds of terrific thoughts about "later" filling his head, he climbed out of the car and entered the old building.

After deactivating the alarm system, he stood listening for a few seconds.

The hushed atmosphere assured him he was the only one there. But since this wasn't the time for taking any chances, he did a quick tour of the main floor and then checked upstairs.

His final stop was Larry's office.

He knocked on the door. When there was no response he unlocked it and stuck his head in.

Satisfied that he was truly alone, he took the back stairs down to the alley door and motioned Dana inside. Then he retraced his steps to Larry's office with her right behind him.

"Where do we start?" he said as she set her purse on the desk.

"Is the filing cabinet locked?" she asked.

"Uh-huh," he said, looking over and seeing that the lock was pushed in.

"The desk is, too," she said, trying the drawers. "I've got a set of picks in my purse. But I'm no expert with them, so this could take a while."

"Or we could get it over with fast," Larry said.

Noah wheeled toward the door, his heart slamming against his rib cage.

Larry was filling the doorway with his bulk. Standing there pointing a large handgun in their direction and looking as if he'd need almost no provocation to use it. So much for this gig involving zero risk.

"Did you take me for a damned idiot?" he snarled, glaring at them.

"Look, Larry," Noah said as evenly as he could.

He got no further because Larry cut him off with an angry wave of his arm and said, "Don't try to give me any bull. I know exactly what's going on.

"Although *you* being here's a surprise," he added. "But I guess Robert told you who Dana really is."

Before he could reply she was saying, "Larry, what do you think—"

"Forget it," he ordered, cutting *her* off this time. "It's not a question of what I *think*. It's what I *know*. I've been listening in on your meetings with Robert."

Noah swore under his breath. How the hell were they going to get out of this?

"What did he figure?" Larry muttered, almost to himself. "That I'd sit around and do nothing while his little detective learned *I* was the one?"

"Do nothing?" Dana repeated. "You call those notes and that stupid doll doing nothing?"

"You should have taken them seriously! If you'd backed off we wouldn't be here now.

"This is all your fault. Maybe Robert suspected

me, but he'd never have pushed so far on his own. He'd have just ridden things out."

"*My* fault? Larry, I've only done what I was paid to do. Maybe you shouldn't have let Robert hire me in the first place."

Noah shot Dana a speculative glance. He assumed she was intentionally trying to keep Larry talking, hoping for a chance to go for her gun. But how would she get enough time to do that when it was in her purse?

"As if I could have *stopped* him from hiring you," Larry was saying.

"Hell, I couldn't even object to the idea too strongly. I had to pretend I wanted to get to the bottom of things, too.

"So I went along with him—then bugged his office to find out exactly what was happening. And when I heard he'd put together the fact that I needed money with—"

"Why didn't you just borrow it from a bank?" Dana interrupted.

"Because banks don't lend you money to keep some loan shark from killing your wife."

"What?" Noah said.

Larry shrugged. "Martha's in big trouble. She was bored after she stopped working. And she started betting on just about everything the bookies had going.

"She went through what was in the bank accounts, then got herself so deep in debt that... When she finally came to me and admitted...

"I've been buying her time, but..." Larry shook his head. "None of that matters now, though. So let's just get going."

"Going where?" Noah said.

"To the third floor." Motioning with his gun, Larry stepped back to let them out of the room.

"Now," he ordered when neither of them moved. "You first, Dana."

"Your purse," Noah said as she started forward.

"Leave it," Larry told her.

Noah could feel his heart begin to pound harder yet. With her gun they at least had a chance. Without it...

Dammit. His job had been to make sure she got in and out of here with no problems. And that sure wasn't what was happening. So he had to think. Had to come up with a plan.

He tried to force his brain into high gear as he fell in step behind her. But all he could think was that Larry was going to kill them.

CHAPTER SIXTEEN

DEAD MAN WALKING.

The movie title had lodged in Dana's brain the moment she'd started up the narrow back staircase, and she couldn't force it out—probably because it fit the situation so perfectly.

Except that there were *two* walking dead. She and Noah.

He was following right behind her, while Larry was bringing up the rear, his gun undoubtedly pointed directly at the center of Noah's back.

Visualizing that made her feel graveyard cold. And made the steel bands of terror that were constricting her chest seem even tighter.

There was absolutely no doubt that Larry intended to shoot them once he got them up to the third floor. Then he'd go and kill Robert. Unless he'd already taken care of that.

Either way, with the three of them gone he'd have eliminated everyone who knew he was the saboteur. And to his mind—

"Open it," he said as she reached the door at the top of the stairs.

When she did, stale air drifted out at her, making her already dry throat even drier.

"Keep walking," he ordered.

She stepped through the doorway, fearfully licking her lips. Larry wasn't going to take his eyes off them for a second. And if he didn't, the chance they'd get out of here alive was awfully small.

So unfair. The phrase skittered painfully through her mind.

Only yesterday, she'd caught herself thinking that her little "partnership" with Noah was going to turn into something serious and lasting. Maybe even permanent. But now...

It would be so unfair if she'd finally found the right man only to lose him.

"Head down to the far end," Larry said.

She forced herself to take another couple of steps into the dimness. Not much light filtered through windows coated with decades of New York grime, but as she moved forward the various shapes became identifiable.

Old furniture. Stacks of tired cartons. Battered filing cabinets.

Dead storage. Robert had told her when she'd asked what was up here. He hadn't been referring to dead *bodies,* though, which was what there'd soon be unless...

Ghosts from the past thirty years. That was something else he'd said. And now Larry was planning to add new ghosts.

But she didn't want to die. And she didn't want Noah to die.

She told herself not to panic. There had to be a way of making Larry see that his plan could never succeed. See that there was no possibility he could murder three people and get away with it.

Yet she understood how he'd have convinced himself there might be.

If he chose some place as secluded as this to kill Robert, if none of their bodies were discovered right away...

And when they were he'd have an alibi for his whereabouts tonight. Martha would give him one. Of course, the police would get at the truth, but...

But none of that mattered. Regardless of what happened down the road it would be too late for her and Noah. Unless she did something right now, in another minute or so they were going to die.

"Larry?" she said, stopping and slowly turning, her fear so strong that it was almost incapacitating.

Noah's expression was as tense as she knew her own must be. Larry looked...*desperate* was the best word.

"What?" he said, aiming his gun past Noah and at her.

"Larry, listen to me. I know a lot about the law. And this is a really bad idea. It's not going to help Martha and you'll end up spending the rest of your life in prison."

"Like I wouldn't for fraud?"

"No, you wouldn't. Fraud isn't murder. And a good lawyer could work something out for you. Could—"

"No! It's gone too far. It's too late for anything else. I've got to take my chances with this.

"All I have to do is buy Martha a little more time. Just until those shares rise. Then it'll be okay."

"No, Larry, it *won't* be okay. I'm supposed to see my father later tonight," she lied. "And he's a cop, so they won't even wait twenty-four hours before they start searching for me. And when they learn Noah's missing, too. And Robert...

"Think, Larry. Where will they look? Who will they suspect?"

He shook his head, still pointing his gun straight at her.

"I'm out of options. This is the only way left. I never meant... But..."

Suddenly Noah spun around and yanked Larry's arm downward. The gun exploded, the roar deafening as the two men grappled for control of it.

Her hands flew behind her, the left one pulling up her shirt, the right grabbing her own gun from where she'd concealed it against the small of her back—her eyes never leaving the struggling men.

Noah was younger, but Larry was so large.

Firing stance now. Holding the gun with both hands and screaming, "Stop! Stop or I'll shoot!"

Her words were only half out when Larry's fist smashed into Noah's face. As he staggered backward

Larry wheeled toward her, aiming his gun at her again.

Oh, Lord. She had to shoot him. If she didn't—

"Drop it!" he ordered.

She swallowed hard.

"I said, drop it!"

She fired.

THE UNIFORMS WHO INITIALLY responded to Noah's 911 call secured the second and third floors of Four Corners as a crime scene. When the police detectives arrived they conducted their interviews downstairs.

It was close to midnight before the two questioning Dana told her she was free to leave. Even so, when she emerged from Chris Vidal's office Noah was waiting for her—his suit jacket slung over his shoulder, his tie hanging from one of its pockets, his shirt-sleeves rolled up.

"Oh, Noah," she whispered, the sight of him causing tears to form.

His right eye was almost completely swollen shut now, and the area around it was purple. But at least someone had cleaned up the gash Larry's ring had made on his cheek. It was bandaged with a large square of gauze and adhesive—which she knew hid more bruising.

"Not pretty, huh?" he said.

"Not exactly picture perfect. But it could have been so much worse. He might have…"

"Yeah, he might have, but he didn't," Noah murmured, gathering her into his arms.

"How about you?" he said after he'd held her close for a minute. "You all right?"

She nodded against his chest, although she still felt very fragile.

"Then let's get out of here," he said, taking her hand. "Get you home."

"Can you see well enough to drive?"

"I'll be fine."

Neither of them spoke again until they'd left the building behind and were stopped for a red light on Tenth Avenue.

Then Noah looked across the car and said, "You know that Larry's going to be okay? That you didn't hit anything vital?"

"Yes. The detectives told me." They'd also told her that Robert was fine. Larry had intended to kill him *after* he'd finished with her and Noah.

"Have you spoken to your uncle?" she asked.

"No. I phoned, but there were detectives at the apartment. Carol said she'd have him get back to me as soon as they left, so they must still be there."

When the traffic began moving again, Dana dug her cell phone out of her purse and said, "I have to call my father. I'll probably be waking him up, but I don't want him hearing from anyone else that there was a shooting at Four Corners."

"You think it'll make the news?"

"In Manhattan? When I didn't hit anything vital?

That's not even filler unless it's a really slow news day.''

Noah gave her a tired smile. ''Your sense of humor's intact. That's got to be a good sign.''

''I guess so. But not making the *Times* doesn't mean we won't make the police grapevine,'' she added, punching in her father's number. ''When the shooter's an ex-cop, as well as a cop's daughter, the boys in blue will be talking.''

Her call did indeed wake Jack Morancy. But once he knew why she was phoning he was very glad she had.

''I'm relieved it's over,'' he said. ''And that you're okay.''

''Me, too.''

''And I want to hear all the details, so are we still on for dinner tomorrow?''

Right. She'd said tomorrow, for sure, in the message she'd left him. ''Absolutely,'' she told him. ''Why don't you come to my place after your shift.''

''Sounds good, darling. See you then.''

Just as she was saying goodbye, Noah's cellular rang—and he spent the rest of the trip talking with Robert, only clicking off as they turned into her street.

''How upset is he?'' she asked.

''Incredibly. Even though he suspected Larry, he was clinging to the hope that it was someone else. And learning that Larry'd intended to kill him...''

She simply nodded. The two of them had been partners for thirty years. There was really nothing more to be said about a betrayal of that magnitude.

Noah found an empty parking space not far from her building and pulled into it. Then he cut the engine, saying, "I'll come up."

She didn't even have to consider whether she wanted him to or not. There wasn't the slightest doubt.

THE MOMENT DANA LOCKED her apartment door Noah took her in his arms and kissed her—a long, tender kiss that made her feel as if they'd managed to seal themselves off from all the evils in the world.

They were safe. And together. She couldn't conceive of a better combination.

When he let her go, she ever so gently touched her fingertips to his bruised face. "Doesn't it hurt to kiss me?" she whispered.

"Only a little."

"Liar," she teased.

"Well…okay, more than a little. What hurts worse, though, is the guy inside my head who won't stop hammering."

"You should have said something. Should have let me drive."

"I thought I was doing okay. The pounding was slowing down, but it seems to be getting worse again."

"Do you want some aspirin?"

"Good idea."

When she started for the kitchen he tossed his suit jacket onto the couch and then followed along, as if he didn't want to let her out of his sight.

She liked that.

And she liked the way he quietly said hello to Doc when the cat sidled into the room. And the way he brushed her forehead with another kiss as she handed him the pill bottle and a glass of water.

Lord, was there anything about him she *didn't* like?

Nothing came to mind.

After downing the aspirin, he said, "Man, I always figured I could take care of myself, but that left hook of Larry's was a lesson in humility. Here I am, still feeling the effects hours later. And when he connected the lights almost went out."

He gazed at her, then added, "If it weren't for you we'd both be dead."

"Noah, if you hadn't made a move I'd never have gotten to my gun. So if it weren't for *you* we'd be dead."

He gave her a weary smile. "Didn't I tell you we'd make a good team?"

"Uh-huh, you did."

She eyed him, suddenly worried that he could have a concussion or something. But when she raised the possibility he said, "I'll be fine. Really. I'm just having some kind of minor relapse."

"Well, at least let's sit down.

"Did you know," she added as they headed into the living room, "that Larry was a boxer in college?"

"Was he?"

She nodded. "That's where his killer punch came from."

"Really?" Noah gingerly lowered himself onto the couch, obviously thinking she might just be saying that.

"Uh-huh. Feel less humiliated?" she said, sitting down beside him.

"Well…yeah, but how did you know about something he did way back when?"

She smiled. "Oh, I know a lot of things."

"You do, don't you," he said quietly. "But do you know I love you?"

His words stopped her midbreath and flooded her with emotion. This wonderful man she was crazy about loved her. That was enough to start the lingering shadow of the horror they'd been through fading—fast.

Noah loved her and…and she loved him. There was no possible way of improving on that situation.

He cleared his throat. "Ah…could you maybe say something?"

"Oh, Noah," she said, certain the grin she felt spreading across her face was making her look like an idiot. "You took me by surprise. But it's a fantastic surprise. I mean…even though it's happened way too fast…"

"Finish it," he said softly.

She was almost afraid to. Afraid it would break the magic spell that had wrapped itself around them. But the way he was looking at her said that *nothing* would break the spell, so she gathered her courage and whispered, "I love you, too."

"Ah," he said. "That's good. No, it's way better than good. It's great." He started to lean closer, then abruptly stopped.

"Noah, are you *certain* you're all right?"

"Yeah. At least I will be. But... This sure isn't the way the scene's supposed to play out, is it?"

"That's okay. Just relax and let the aspirin work."

He reached for her hand, then rested his head against the couch and shut his eyes.

She studied him—the firm cords of muscles in his neck, the breadth of his shoulders, the way his shirt clung to his chest, the dark hairs on his arms where his sleeves were rolled up. And his face.

Even bruised and bandaged he was a gorgeous-looking man. Quite possibly, the most gorgeous in the entire world. Well...the entire city, for sure. There wasn't any debating that.

And she was awfully glad that Larry hadn't broken anything. Like Noah's jaw. Or his straight, even nose.

She suspected he'd end up with a scar where the ring bit into his cheek, but they were both just *so* fortunate to still be alive, let alone basically okay. She wasn't sure that had entirely sunk in yet.

"The hammering's slowing down again," Noah said without opening his eyes.

"Good."

He was quiet for a couple of minutes more, then

he focused on her and said, ''Four Corners is going to be closed until the police are through there. Which they told Robert will be at least two or three days.

''At any rate, he said not to even think about business tomorrow.''

''Well, my job is basically done, anyway. Aside from writing up a final report—which I can't imagine he cares much about.''

''No, and he said that after what we'd been through tonight we should just take it easy for a day or two. He sounded as concerned about you as me, by the way.''

''Really? He's a nice man.''

Noah nodded. ''I don't imagine what he had in mind was us taking it easy together, but that's what *I'm* thinking.''

She smiled. ''I like the way you think. My dad's coming for dinner tomorrow,'' she added as she remembered. ''That's good, though. The two of you can get to know each other better.''

And once they did, her father would see that there was no earthly reason not to like Noah. Or maybe she was only imagining that he didn't.

''But what about the daytime?'' she said. ''Anything particular in mind?''

''Well, as you said, your job there's basically done. Which means we don't have to worry about being circumspect any longer. Do we?''

She couldn't help smiling. ''No, I guess we don't.''

The look that response generated sent a hot rush

through her—and made her hope the aspirin really *was* helping.

When he leaned closer and nuzzled her ear, she decided it must be. And thank heavens, because she desperately wanted this scene to play out the way it was supposed to.

"So," he said quietly, "if we're going to spend tomorrow together, does it make any sense for me to go home?"

Her heartbeat accelerated into overdrive. "It wouldn't be the most efficient plan, would it?"

He kissed the hollow at the base of her throat. "No. It wouldn't be efficient at all.

"And you know what?" he added, taking both her hands in his and pulling her to her feet.

"What?" she whispered.

"You were wrong when you said this has happened way too fast."

"I was?"

"Uh-huh. When something's right, it's right— whether it takes months to realize, or weeks, or only a few days."

He stood gazing into her very soul, making her certain that what he'd just told her was true.

Then he said, "I think we've been looking for each other a long time, Dana. Without realizing it. That explains why neither of us have ever married. Subconsciously, we've both known to wait."

Her heart had revved up to a hundred beats a minute and her thoughts were racing every bit as rapidly.

Maybe that *did* explain why she'd never found a man who was quite right for her. Until now.

Noah slid his fingers up under the loose bottom edge of her shirt and around to her spine, the warmth of his touch on her bare skin turning her liquid inside.

"Checking for your gun," he said, resting his palms against the small of her back.

"It's not there."

"Just making sure, because I didn't know it was there earlier. I thought it was in your purse."

"I took it out after you went into the building."

"Yeah, I deduced that."

"Deduced." She smiled. "That's a very detective word."

"Well, it's what I did. But not until after you'd shot Larry. Up until then, I was sure we were toast."

For a moment she was certain he was going to ask how she felt about the shooting. She'd been expecting him to almost from the time she'd pulled the trigger.

But he must have sensed that she still wasn't ready to really think about those feelings, let alone talk about them, because instead of saying another word he simply wrapped his arm around her waist and started toward the bedroom.

"Noah?" she said, hesitating.

He looked at her.

She rested her fingers against the swollen side of his face once more. "Are you sure this will be okay?"

He smiled at her. "I'm sure it'll be a quantum leap better than okay."

When he started forward again, she didn't resist. That was the last thing she wanted to do now that she finally *had* found the right man.

Stopping at the bedroom doorway, he gave her another tender kiss. Then he picked her up and carried her to the bed.

"I want to make love to you all night long," he said as he laid her down.

He took a condom package from his pocket and tossed it onto the bedside table, then he stretched out beside her, the mattress creaking under the added weight.

"Since the first time I saw you," he murmured, "I've been imagining what this would be like. Imagining what your skin would taste like. How soft it would feel against mine."

Framing her face with his hands, he kissed her again, his mouth warm and inviting, his kiss more sensual than before, more greedy.

She slid her palms slowly down his chest, loving the hardness of his body and the way his nearness was making her feel a steamy anticipation inside.

Then he eased back a bit and met her gaze.

The only light in the bedroom came from the tiny green dot on her computer and the glow of the night outside. Reflected light of the city. Harsh on the streets, dim in her room.

Just enough to let her see that Noah didn't take his

eyes from her face as he undid the buttons of her shirt. Unhooked the front clasp of her bra. Pushed the fabric off her shoulders and down her arms.

Slowly, he cupped her breasts, grazing her nipples with his thumbs. Making them hard. Making her moan with pleasure. Making her begin to squirm. Watching her become more and more aroused by his touch.

In a way, it was disconcerting. Yet his watching, his seeing what he was doing to her, made her hotter still.

Heat balled low inside her, intensifying her desire until she was aware of nothing else. Nothing but it and her need to have Noah satisfy it.

"As soft as I imagined," he murmured at last. Then he lowered his head and took a nipple in his mouth.

The hot, wet sensation was like an electric jolt; she felt as if she was coming apart at the seams.

"Oh, Noah," she whispered, clutching his shoulders as he moved lower to ease her slacks and panties off.

Seconds later, his own clothes were on the floor and she was kissing him again—while her hands roamed over his chest, his back, his hips.

She loved his taste, his smell. Wanted to touch every naked inch of him, to kiss every naked inch of him. Wanted him inside her so badly that the desperate throbbing between her legs was painful.

He slid his hand there and she almost exploded.

Then he shifted lower and began kissing her there…and she did.

Her orgasm was all-consuming. Tremor after tremor seized her, keeping her from breathing, bringing tears to her eyes and making her whimper as if something inside her was trying to escape but couldn't.

And then Noah was inside her and the tremors grew impossibly stronger. Waves of blinding sensation pulsed through her and she could only cling to Noah.

Until the tremors finally began to lessen. Until she was able to gasp tiny breaths. Until Noah had collapsed on top of her, his chest heaving as he, too, gasped for air.

CHAPTER SEVENTEEN

THE SECOND TIME THEY MADE love it was far less frantic. The third, it was almost in slow motion with the early light of morning stealing into Dana's bedroom.

Afterward, she lay in Noah's arms, not quite able to erase a smile from her face.

"Can I ask you something?" he said quietly.

"Of course."

"It's about last night. About Larry.

"Don't tense up on me," he added—even before she realized she'd stiffened and her smile was gone. "I just…"

While he was choosing his next words, she began a deep-breathing exercise the department shrink had taught her way back in what almost seemed another lifetime.

"When you told me what happened with that kid," Noah finally continued, "you were so upset and… Even though the circumstances were different… Shooting someone again… Are you okay with it?"

The question gave her pause, because up until this minute she'd been doing a good job of avoiding thinking about it.

But now that Noah had pressed…well, either she wasn't actually doing too badly, mentally speaking, or the breathing exercise had helped far more than it usually did.

"Dana?"

She snuggled as closely to him as she could and said, "I'm trying to sort out how I feel."

"Take all the time you need," he murmured, trailing his fingers down her bare arm.

That was enough to bring her smile back—momentarily, at least.

"You know," she told him at last, "when most children are little, and their parents are trying to teach them right from wrong, one of the wrongs is hurting other people. And killing is so far beyond hurting…

"But when your father's a cop, you hear a modified version. It's wrong to hurt other people. Or kill them. *Unless* there's a good reason. Unless they're evil. Or they're threatening someone. Or…

"Well, you understand what I'm saying. The message is that *sometimes* it's okay. Which is the same message recruits get at the academy. And officers get on the job."

"Yeah, I understand." He punctuated his reply by kissing her bare shoulder.

"You're distracting me."

"Sorry."

"Don't be. I like it. But…when I shot that kid I thought I was doing the right thing. The only thing I *could* do. Then, when I learned his gun wasn't real…

"That was a big part of why I wasn't sure I'd ever be able to use my weapon again. Because I'd thought I was doing the right thing but it turned out so, so wrong."

Her voice must have told Noah she was becoming emotional because he quietly said, "Dana, you didn't know his gun wasn't real, remember?"

She nodded, wondering how many times people had said that to her, how many times she'd said it to herself.

"No, I didn't know. But the point is that afterward I'd stopped feeling I could trust my own judgment. Whereas, last night... I *knew* I was right. I mean, I didn't mistrust myself. I *knew* that shooting Larry was the only thing I could do."

"And so you did it," Noah said softly.

"Yes. Even though I'd spent five years not sure if...

"Noah, maybe I'll never fire a gun again in my entire life. In fact, I seriously hope I won't. But I feel better for being certain that I can if I have to. So...

"In a way it's ironic, isn't it. Shooting someone is an awful experience. It's actually pretty common for a police officer to suffer post-traumatic stress afterward, even when the circumstances aren't as horrible as mine were.

"But last night...I don't feel good about what happened. That isn't what I'm trying to say. Yet it's as if by making myself shoot Larry I somehow exorcised my demons—destroyed the self-doubt I'd had for so long."

Noah brushed her hair back from her face, then said, "And the rest of the baggage? Having to leave the force? Figuring you'd disappointed your father?"

"I'm not really sure," she admitted. "I haven't thought that far. But when I spoke to him last night he sounded pretty darned proud of me. So maybe...maybe you were right. Maybe I should talk to him about the other.

"As for quitting...I liked being a cop. But I'm happy with what I'm doing now. Probably more happy."

"You know," Noah whispered against her ear, "I'm happy with what you're doing now, too. With what you're doing *right* now," he added—as if he thought she might miss his meaning. "So maybe we could just keep on doing it forever."

Forever. As in long-term commitment.

"You think?" she whispered back, smiling once more.

"It's definitely something to consider," he said before he kissed her.

THEY SPENT THE DAY doing all sorts of things Noah hadn't done in years.

Had breakfast in bed, lunch at the Russian Tea Room (even though he had to slip the maître d' a hundred bucks to get a table without a reservation), ate ice-cream cones in Central Park and wandered hand-in-hand down Fifth Avenue—drinking in the sights and sounds of the city and gawking at display windows like a couple of tourists.

Of course, the first few times he caught his reflection it jolted him. He'd only taken one punch, yet he looked as if he'd gone ten rounds at Gold's Gym. Which made him think he was lucky he hadn't had to tip *two* hundred bucks for that table.

But after the first little while he stopped paying attention to his reflection. And by the time they reached Tiffany's windows...

Well, normally he didn't have the slightest interest in jewelry. Today, though, he found himself staring at the diamond rings and wondering just how soon he could ask Dana to marry him. Without her thinking it was *too* soon.

Not that he hadn't already been edging around the subject. But he didn't want to come straight out with the question until the time was right.

He just hoped that wouldn't be too long from now, because he couldn't remember ever enjoying himself more than he had today. And he knew the reason was that he'd been with Dana. And that had to mean the sooner he was with her permanently, the better.

By the time they headed back to her apartment it was so late that they cheated on the cooking and stopped by a place that catered great food. Neither of them really needed to eat anything more for a week, but they could hardly starve her father.

After they'd arrived home and fed Doc, Dana

started to set the table while he called Robert to get an update on what had been happening. When he clicked off fifteen minutes later, she eyed him expectantly.

"He went to the hospital to see Larry this morning," he told her. "To hear the entire story from him.

"But Larry's lawyer had left strict orders that *nobody* was to talk to him. And since Larry's under police guard there was no way around that. So he paid Martha a visit."

"Oh? And that got him…?"

"Most of the details he wanted."

"Then she was in on the plan?"

He shrugged. "According to her, she was only *aware* of it. She didn't actually play any part.

"Robert figures that's debatable. What he's gathered from the police is that they might charge her as an accessory. They're still collecting evidence."

"But if she *wasn't* involved, why would Larry have filled her in? Wouldn't it have occurred to him that he was implicating her?"

"It might not have. And if she honestly wasn't playing an active role, then maybe he was only telling her what he was doing to reassure her—so she'd know he was working on getting her out of the mess she was in."

"But then she just willingly spilled everything to Robert? That doesn't ring true."

"Well, it sounded as if he did a good job of faking

her out. He pretended he already knew everything Larry had done and how.''

''Good for him.''

''Plus, she was probably too upset to be thinking straight.''

''I guess. When your husband's likely to spend the rest of his life in prison…''

''And now the only way she'll be able to pay off the loan shark will be by selling their apartment. That can't be helping her mental heath.''

Dana nodded. ''You're right. She had more important things to worry about than what she was saying to Robert. But what did he learn?''

''Well, we'd already figured out most of it. The stock manipulation. The friend who was buying up shares while the price was depressed. He *did* get the true story about the missing containers, though.''

''Which is?''

''Larry made a deal with the boat captain to only unload four. If Tony Zicco had realized there were supposed to be six, the captain would have just claimed an innocent mistake.

''Oh, and to improve the odds that the *mistake* wouldn't be noticed, Larry made sure Stu Refkin was gone before the cargo ship docked.''

''How?''

''He had someone, ostensibly a guy from another company, call Stu and say they were looking for a warehouse manager and had heard great things about him. The salary this guy mentioned was fantastic, so Stu went for an interview.''

"On that Friday afternoon.''

"Right.''

"And that explains why he lied about going to meet his wife. He didn't want anyone at Four Corners to know he'd been interviewing for another job.'' Dana slowly shook her head. "Larry didn't miss a trick, did he?''

"Not until last night.''

THE EVENING HADN'T GONE WELL, which had Dana very worried.

Her feeling that her father didn't like Noah had started growing stronger as soon as he'd arrived—even though she wasn't able to put her finger on anything specific.

Jack Morancy had been polite enough, and had shown obvious interest in all the details of last night's misadventure, but she sensed an uncomfortable undercurrent that really bothered her.

She was in love with Noah. Madly, insanely in love with him. She'd never experienced anything even remotely like it before. And the thought that her father was *not* happy about their relationship, whatever his reason...

"Well,'' Noah said, giving her a reluctant glance, "I guess I'd better take off.''

She didn't want him to go. She'd been expecting him to spend the night again. But it was eleven o'clock and her father had shown absolutely no sign of leaving.

He'd been outwaiting Noah. She knew that was his game. But why was he playing it? What had he decided was wrong with the man she loved?

When she saw Noah to the door, he murmured, "I was hoping to stay."

"Great minds," she whispered.

"I'll call you in the morning."

"Good."

She shut the door behind him, then wandered back into the living room, sat down beside her father and said, "Dad, what's the matter?"

He shook his head, finally saying, "There's something I've got to tell you."

Oh, Lord. Had she guessed wrong? Maybe the funk he'd been in recently had nothing to do with Noah. Maybe he was seriously ill or something.

Cancer. Her mother had died of cancer. Was he going to tell her that he had it now? That possibility started her stomach churning.

"What?" she made herself say.

"I...Dana, you know I love you more than anyone else on earth."

"Of course I do," she murmured. "I love you, too."

He paused, then said, "This is hard, darling."

Oh, please. Please don't let it be cancer.

"In fact, it's one of the hardest things I've ever had to do."

''What?'' she said again, the word barely audible this time.

''Dana...I'm not your biological father.''

She gazed at him in stunned silence, certain she wouldn't be able to utter a word if she tried.

At last, she managed to say, ''Explain.''

He exhaled slowly. ''Well, you know your mother and I started dating in high school.''

''Uh-huh.''

''Then we got engaged when I joined the force. But a few months after that we had a stupid argument. And she gave me my ring back.''

''I've never heard this story,'' she said.

''No. Because...you'll understand why in a minute.

''We didn't get together again for about six months. And during that time she started dating someone else. And...Dana, the thing is, she got pregnant.''

She simply stared at her father, aware what he was saying wasn't sinking in too well.

''With me?'' she whispered at last.

''Yes.''

''My mother...''

Her mother had slept with someone other than her father. That probably shouldn't astonish her, but the impression her mother had always given her was—

''She said she only started going with him to show me,'' her father said. ''But...things happen, Dana. You know that.''

''Yes,'' she managed to say. But how could *this* particular thing...

Jack Morancy was her father. And her mother had been crazy about him. Maybe he somehow had this wrong.

But he was nodding that it was true.

"At any rate," he continued, "when she told this guy she was pregnant he wanted her to have an abortion. Well, she wasn't going to do that and they broke up.

"Then, a few days later, she called me. She always claimed she didn't expect anything more from me than a shoulder to cry on. But I still loved her. And she still loved me.

"So we decided we'd get married and just never tell anyone that I wasn't your real father."

"Oh, Dad," she murmured, her eyes filling with tears. "You *are* my real father."

He gave her a wan smile. "That's the way I've always felt, Dana. I've always loved you as if you were my own flesh and blood. And the fact that your mother and I never had...more children, just made you so special. And...well, I always tried to be the best father I could."

"Oh, Daddy," she said, hugging him tightly as her tears spilled over. "You've been the best father in the world."

He patted her back while she cried, the way he'd done when she was a little girl, until she pulled herself together enough to look at him again and say, "But why did you tell me? After you kept it a secret all those years?"

Jack Morancy raked his fingers through his hair. "Because," he said at last, "there was no real reason you ever had to know before. But now there is. Dana…your biological father is Robert Haine."

"Robert Haine," she repeated, feeling totally stunned all over again.

Her father sat watching her, clearly waiting for her to put something together. But she didn't know what. And then she did.

"Oh, Lord," she whispered, her insides suddenly hurting. "He's Noah's uncle, so Noah is my cousin."

"That's right, darling. I'd give anything not to have to shock you like this, but…"

She wrapped her arms around her chest, still reeling from the news that her father wasn't actually her father and now trying to digest the Noah part.

"You see—"

She did her utmost to concentrate as he began speaking once more, but she could barely make out what he was saying because her ears were ringing.

It was something about how, after she'd first mentioned Robert's name, he'd run a check to make sure that it was the *same* Robert Haine.

Listen, she ordered herself. Pay attention. Keep your emotions in check.

The last one was impossible, but she tried as hard as she could.

"That's when I knew I had to tell you," her father continued. "Because the other day, the very first time

I saw you and Noah together…the way you look at each other…''

''Is it that obvious?'' she murmured.

''Uh-huh.''

But of course it was. Noah was the love of her life. Now, though…

Just pay attention, she told herself again. *Get the facts straight. Save the processing for later.*

''Dana, of all the fellows you've ever dated…well, I've never seen you look at any of them that way. And…

''Darling, I know how hard it is when you get hit with something like this out of the blue, but things aren't as bad as you might be thinking.

''If you and Noah got to the stage of… Well, it's legal for first cousins to marry in New York State. I checked on that. But…

''I figured I *had* to tell you about this, Dana. About your mother and Robert, I mean. That there was just no way around it.''

''No. You were right. You had to tell me.''

Her mother and Robert. Her and Noah. Cousins marrying.

Marriage. Yes, that was where things were heading.

Or maybe *had* been heading was more accurate. She didn't know up from down right now, let alone what this meant to her and Noah.

Only this morning he'd been thinking marriage. He wasn't the kind of man who'd use the word *forever* if that wasn't what he meant.

And she hadn't missed him staring at those diamond rings in Tiffany's window, either.

Now, though…

No, she couldn't even begin to sort through the ramifications of this at the moment.

She needed time. Had to put the…situation—yes, it was definitely a situation—on hold until later. Until all this was clear in her mind. Better to focus on something else for the moment.

Robert. Okay. Focus on him. Her *real* father. Who *wasn't* her real father because Jack Morancy was.

She licked her dry lips, then said, "Does Robert know I'm his daughter?"

"I think he has to."

She nodded, as if that made perfect sense to her. But *none* of this was making even imperfect sense. It was all one big horrible jumble.

"After Robert and your mother broke up," her father continued, "she never heard from him again. But he *did* know she was pregnant. And the fact that he chose to hire you…

"He must have either kept track of you all this time or he decided to find you at some point. Otherwise…

"Well, it would be the coincidence of the century if he'd needed a P.I. and just happened to pick you."

"So he has to know that Noah and I are cousins." Logical statement. Good. Her mind was starting to put things together.

Her father nodded. "Yes, obviously. But does he know that the two of you…?"

"No. We've been very careful around Four Corners."

There was a long silence while she took a serious stab at sorting everything out in her head. But she still wasn't thinking clearly and there was an awful lot to sort.

At length her father said, "Dana, if this hadn't happened I'd never have told you the truth. Your whole life, I've been afraid that if you found out it would make things different between us."

Her eyes filled with tears again. "Oh, Daddy, nothing would ever change how much I love you. You were always there for me, and..."

Since her throat was too tight to say more, she simply wrapped her arms around his neck and clung to him again.

DANA DIDN'T BOTHER going to bed after her father left. There was no point when she knew she'd never sleep. Not with her emotions in total overload and a thousand different thoughts warring for her attention.

She just sat on the couch with Doc beside her, trying to work her way through the situation.

A father was somebody who taught you how to ride a bike and throw a ball, who read you bedtime stories and took you to Yankees games. Who told you the boy who dumped you in tenth grade didn't have a brain in his head. And wouldn't have been half good enough for you even if he did.

Then, when you were older, it was your father who

took five rolls of pictures at your graduation. Your father who sat with you in the hospital, holding your hand while your mother—the only woman he'd ever loved—was dying.

She swallowed hard at that memory, and there were a thousand more. Things they'd done together, times they'd shared.

There was absolutely no doubt that Jack Morancy *was* her real father. And as soon as the shock of his bombshell had worn off a little she'd been certain that part wouldn't be a problem for either of them. They'd carry on as always. Father and daughter.

But Noah…oh, Lord, what about Noah and her? How would he react when she told him? How would he feel?

Of course, she wasn't even sure how she felt— aside from being so upset that she was sort of hollow inside.

It made sense to start there, she told herself. By figuring out where *she* was, feelings-wise.

Yet with her mind still spinning, how could she hope to figure out anything?

Cousins. First cousins. If she'd known that's what they were in the beginning would she ever…

No, she wouldn't have.

She pictured him. His fabulous smile. Looking at her with love in his eyes.

But if she'd known the truth from the start…

Yet if it was legal for first cousins to marry, then why did she feel that there was something…

Various words began flashing before her eyes, each making her less happy than the one before.

Inappropriate. Unseemly. Indelicate.

She closed the cover on her mental thesaurus before the words got any worse, then simply sat stroking Doc and hoping that everything tumbling around in her head would magically freeze-frame into a perfectly clear picture.

When that didn't happen, she decided it might help to get a factual perspective. Because at this point she was awfully long on angst and awfully short on objectivity.

After giving Doc's ear a final rub, she headed into her bedroom and sat down at the computer.

She barely breathed while it connected to the Net and the search engine she called up appeared on screen.

Then, her fingers trembling, she typed in *cousins and marriage.*

There was a ton of hits.

She scanned a few, then came to an article that was chock-full of information.

The law of the Roman Catholic Church in the Middle Ages, she read, prohibited first-cousin marriages.

Bad.

But only without prior dispensation, and dispensations were relatively easy to obtain.

Maybe not so bad, then.

Such marriages weren't uncommon in the 1800s.

Charles Darwin married his first cousin. As did Queen Victoria.

Promising.

However, after about 1850 a general prejudice against first-cousin marriages developed in American society, which was still held by many in the U.S. today.

Uh-oh.

Then she got to the next section of the article and winced. Her dad was right. The marriages were legal in New York State. But thirty states prohibited them.

Thirty. Thirty out of fifty. *Very bad.*

On the other hand, in Europe, there wasn't a single country where they were illegal.

This was not making rational sense, didn't fit neatly into any logical drawer. And then she got to the *really* awful part.

First cousins, she read, run twice the risk of producing unhealthy offspring as parents who are unrelated.

She forced herself to read the statement again, her blood turning to ice as she did.

That wasn't a risk she could conceivably imagine herself taking.

CHAPTER EIGHTEEN

NOAH HADN'T SLEPT WELL.

He'd been trying to convince himself that was only because he was still keyed up from the excitement with Larry. And because he'd been totally buzzed since the moment he'd realized he wanted to marry Dana. But he knew there was a "worry" component involved as well.

Jack Morancy didn't like him.

The first time they'd met, he'd assumed Jack was just perturbed at finding a strange man in his daughter's apartment.

Last night, however, it had been obvious there was more to it than that.

For whatever reason, Jack didn't want him around Dana. And since she adored her father, his approval had to be important to her. Which meant...

Well, that was where he ran into a big field of uncertainty. He didn't know exactly how much Jack's disapproval would bother her, but the smart thing for him to do would be to win Jack over.

The question was how.

He glanced at the clock again, reminding himself that just because he was up this early didn't mean

Dana was. Yet he had to find out what had happened after he'd left last night.

What if Jack had done his best to convince her that Noah Haine wasn't the right man for her? What if…?

But asking himself questions he couldn't answer was futile, so he picked up the phone and punched in her number.

"Hi," he said when she answered.

"Oh…Noah…hi."

His heart sank to the pit of his stomach. Three words and he could tell something was seriously wrong. It hardly took a mind reader to know what.

"I didn't wake you, did I?" he asked as casually as he could.

"No. I was up."

"Ah. Good. Your phone had already started ringing before I thought maybe I should have waited—that your father might not have left until really late and you were sleeping in."

He willed her to say that Jack Morancy had left two seconds after he had. Instead, she said, "No, actually there's something I have to do this morning, so…"

Oh, man, this was *really* bad.

Last night, when he'd told her he'd been hoping to stay, she'd said that's what she'd been hoping, too. And she hadn't mentioned a word about having plans for the morning.

"Well, let's get together for lunch, then," he suggested.

"Lunch," she repeated, as if it were a foreign word.

"Uh-huh. How about I meet you at noon? You name the place."

There was a long silence before she said, "I'll be on the Upper East Side, so do you know that French restaurant just down Seventieth from the Frick? The name isn't coming to mind, but it's got a blue-and-white-striped awning."

"Yeah, I know the one you mean. I'll see you there at twelve."

There was another silence. "Noah, there's a chance I won't be able to make it. If I can't, I'll call your cell."

Before he could say another word, she was gone.

DANA HUNG UP THE PHONE, her throat so tight that she'd done well to get through the conversation without breaking down.

She'd ended up spending almost the entire night on the Internet, and the more articles she'd read, the more thinking she'd done....

She desperately wished she could have asked Noah to come straight over. And that when he'd arrived she could have just held him and never let him go. But things were hardly that simple.

Now, *there* was an understatement. Things could hardly be more complicated. And when she told him...

Shaking her head, she wondered for the millionth time how he'd react.

The other day, he'd mentioned that he wanted children. So even if he didn't share the "general prejudice" against first-cousin marriages that had been referred to a dozen different ways in those articles...

Twice the risk of producing unhealthy offspring.

That was the *real* kicker. The one that had nothing to do with prejudice or attitude or anything else that was only in their heads. The one that was genetic, that they had absolutely no way of changing.

Yet maybe, just maybe...

She went into the bedroom and glanced at the piece of paper with Robert Haine's address and phone number on it.

When she'd originally noted them, as part of the "client homework" she'd done on the key players at Four Corners, she'd never imagined she'd be paying him a home visit. But things were vastly different than they'd been in the beginning.

She told herself she should call and make sure he was there. But if she did he'd want to know what was so urgent, and she couldn't get into that on the phone.

Besides, the police would still have Four Corners sealed off, so the odds were good that he'd be home. If he wasn't...

Well, wherever he was, she *had* to see him before she saw Noah again.

She finished getting ready, trying not to let herself

think that the hope she was clinging to was incredibly faint.

Her father rarely made mistakes. So the check he'd run on Robert, establishing that he was the same Robert Haine her mother had known...

Known. She still hadn't quite gotten her head around the fact that her mother and Robert...

Telling herself she would in time, she turned her thoughts back to that check.

If there'd been an error in the database...

After all, computers weren't infallible. And surely there had to be more than one man named Robert Haine. So it was *possible* that... Or maybe...

She knew she was really reaching, but maybe her mother had only *claimed* Robert was her father.

Not that she'd been able to come up with any logical reason her mother would have lied about who the father of her child was, but...

Grasping at straws, an imaginary voice whispered. She knew she was. That was all she had, though.

After glancing into the mirror a final time, she gave Doc his morning treat—then headed out and hailed a cab. Less than half an hour later she was standing in the marble-floored foyer of Robert's Upper East Side apartment building.

"Is he expecting you?" the concierge asked.

"No, but I'm a business associate."

As the man called Robert's apartment, she wondered what he'd have thought if she'd told him she was Robert's long-lost daughter.

"You can go right up, Ms. Morancy. It's apartment 703."

"Thank you."

As she walked across to the elevators, her knees felt only a little weak. By the time she reached the seventh floor, they'd progressed from "a little" to "incredibly."

Robert opened his door before she'd even knocked, greeting her with a smile and inviting her in.

"This is my wife, Carol," he said, introducing her to the attractive woman whom Dana knew must be wondering what she was doing here.

"You look very together for someone who was almost killed the other night," Carol told her.

"I'm glad." She resisted the impulse to say that looks could be deceiving. Very together was definitely not how she felt.

"I wonder," she said when Robert motioned her toward the living room, "if we could speak privately?"

"Of course. In my study."

He led the way to a mahogany-paneled room that put her in mind of a miniature private club, then closed the door and gestured her to sit, saying, "I told Noah that neither of you should even think about Four Corners for a couple of days."

"That's not why I'm here." She clasped her hands to keep them from trembling.

"Oh?" He sat down himself and eyed her curiously.

She took a deep breath, gathering all her courage, then said, "I have a question."

"Yes?"

It was hard to force the words out, but she finally managed to say, "Am I your daughter?"

His face lost a shade of color.

She waited, not breathing, studying him, searching for features they might have in common.

Not his eyes, she had her mother's eyes. But maybe her chin and nose were like his... Maybe.

"Yes, you are," he said at last.

So that was it, then. No mistake. She shared genes with Noah.

She felt like crying.

She wasn't going to let herself.

Not in front of Robert.

"How did you find out?" he asked quietly.

"My father told me."

Robert hesitated a beat, then said, "Jack Morancy."

"Yes."

"Why? After all this time?"

She shook her head. The why was between her and Noah. And since Robert wasn't even aware there *was* a "her and Noah," there was no point in getting into it with him.

"The reason doesn't matter," she said, her voice tight. "But...tell me your side of the story."

He slowly rubbed his jaw, then said, "There isn't much to tell. Your mother and I dated for a few months and she got pregnant. We...we weren't in love. I mean, I really liked her, but..."

"But you didn't want to marry her."

"Dana...she didn't want to marry me, either."

"So *your* solution to her problem was that she should have an abortion."

"Oh, jeez...I...it wasn't my *solution*. Is that what Jack told you?"

When she didn't reply, Robert said, "It was an option, that's all. And I didn't tell her I thought it was what she should do. I told her that if it was what she wanted I'd pay for it."

"I see," she said. Then she sat staring at her shoes, fiercely blinking back tears.

Robert's version wasn't *exactly* the same as her father's, and with her mother gone she was never going to know the precise truth. But how much did that really matter?

"Dana," he said at last, "we're talking about something that happened more than thirty years ago. Your mother and I were younger than you are now. We were two people in our twenties. With, as you called it, a problem. And..."

"And?"

"And we discussed abortion. We discussed putting you up for adoption. We discussed her raising you on her own, and I told her that if she decided to do that I'd pay child support.

"Actually, we even did discuss marriage. But, as I said, she didn't want to marry me."

She met his gaze. "What if she had? Would you have married her? Would *you* have raised me, rather than Jack Morancy?"

"I honestly don't know. It wasn't a decision I had to make."

"So then? You talked about the options, and then?"

"She said she'd call me after she'd had time to think."

"And did she?"

"Yes."

"And?"

"She told me she'd decided to marry Jack and they were going to pretend you were his. And she swore me to secrecy."

Dana slowly nodded. According to her father, after her mother and Robert had broken up they'd never spoken to each other again.

Obviously, her mother had kept a few things to herself—probably thinking that Jack wouldn't like the idea of her having anything at all more to do with Robert. Which, given the circumstances, had likely been true.

"Dana...I hope you don't hate me."

Did she?

She considered his words briefly and concluded she didn't. She'd actually liked him, as a person, from the beginning. Oh, she'd been thinking he was a rotter after hearing her father's telling of the story, but now... And Robert hadn't *intentionally* caused her problem with Noah.

When she shook her head, he quietly said, "I'm glad. I'm not sure I deserve it, but I'm glad."

There was a silence and then he said, "I always wondered about you, Dana. But I'd promised your mother I'd never make contact.

"I...kind of kept track of you, though."

"Really?" she said, meeting his gaze once more. "How?"

"A private investigator. It was nothing much. Just a brief report now and then. How you were doing in school. That you became a cop, then a P.I. Sometimes little things, like your getting a cat."

"That was how you knew his name."

Robert looked puzzled.

"It doesn't matter," she told him.

"Well...in any event, a long time ago I started wishing I could meet you. See what you were like. Maybe that was because I'd never had a family, and I'd look at Larry with his three kids and...

"I guess it's just one of those things you wish for without knowing exactly why. But, obviously, I didn't do anything about it."

"You'd promised my mother."

"Right. And even if I hadn't...well, it was clear from the reports that Jack was a good father and...I couldn't suddenly just barge into your life.

"But then the problems started at the company.

And when I decided I needed an investigator...I couldn't resist satisfying my curiosity.

"Although, if I'd had any idea it would lead to your almost getting killed..."

After another silence he said, "Dana, whatever Jack's reason for telling you, I assume it had something to do with the fact I hired you. So I'm sorry. I didn't mean to hurt you."

She nodded, not even wanting to think about just how bad the hurt might end up being.

DANA HAD LEFT HERSELF an out by warning Noah that she might not be able to meet him.

She hadn't known whether or not she'd be up to it after seeing Robert—and she still wasn't sure. But she knew she'd be an emotional wreck until they'd talked, so...

Of course, she might be an even worse wreck afterward. There was no possible way she could simply not tell him, though. And since there wasn't, the sensible thing was to just get it over with.

Fine, in theory. In reality, she was standing outside Henri's Bistro, unable to force herself to reach for the door handle and certain that lunch wasn't an even remotely good idea.

Sooner might be better than later, but not in a public place. Not when she had a horrible feeling that she'd end up in tears.

She was just about to turn and flee, when the door opened from inside and Noah was standing there.

"Dana? What's the matter?" he said, stepping out onto the sidewalk.

Oh, Lord. Now she was trapped. "I...we have to talk. But not in there."

"All right," he said, his expression concerned. "My car's down the block. Or would you rather just walk a bit?"

"Yes. Let's walk."

When he took her hand, she didn't know whether to pull it away or not.

She loved this man. Deeply and desperately. But she just didn't know...

"Are you going to tell me what the problem is?" he asked quietly.

"Yes," she made herself say. "I...after you left last night, my father told me something...earth-shattering."

Right. That wasn't too strong a word. Not at all.

"Oh?"

She had to repeat the sentence three times in her head before it would finally come out. "He isn't my biological father."

"What?" Noah gazed at her for a moment, then simply pulled her into his arms.

She pressed her cheek against his chest and stood listening to the solid thudding of his heart—wishing she could stop right there. Stay right here. Never move and not tell him anything more.

"I knew something was wrong," he said against

her hair. "But I thought… Well, that doesn't matter. Tell me the rest."

The rest. The even worse part that might mean the end for them.

"Noah…" She made herself step away so she could look at him. "Robert is my father."

"What?" he said again. "You mean my uncle? That Robert?"

She swallowed hard and nodded.

"But how… Seriously?"

"Yes. He and my mother…"

"Man, oh, man. Uncle Robert? Your father? That's unbelievable. But…Dana, just how upset are you?"

The penny hadn't dropped. He didn't realize what this meant.

Again, she had trouble forcing the words out. "That makes us cousins," she said at last.

"Well…yeah, I guess it does. But you didn't answer my question. I know how close you are to your dad, so you must be feeling—"

"Noah, yes, I'm upset about that. Very upset. But you and I are cousins, and—"

"Nothing to worry about there."

"Nothing? Oh, Noah, if you really love me—"

"*If* I really love you? Dana, I want to marry you. That's how much I really love you."

"But it's not that easy anymore! Maybe it's not even a possibility!"

Her words began pouring out now, tumbling all over themselves as she started to tell him about the articles. The shared genes. How it wouldn't be safe to have children.

"Hey," he interrupted. "None of that matters."

"But it does! You don't—"

"Dana." He grabbed her arms and met her gaze. "Listen to me. I'm adopted."

She stared at him.

He smiled. "So there's no problem. I don't have any of the same genes as Robert."

"Adopted."

"Uh-huh. When I was only a few weeks old."

She didn't know whether to laugh or cry. She'd just gone through the most agonizing night of her entire life because…

"It didn't occur to you to mention that before now?" she said.

"I…no. I hardly ever think about it. I mean, I'd have told you at some point, but it's not something I—"

"Oh, Noah," she murmured.

Then she wrapped her arms around his neck and kissed him. She'd already heard everything she needed to.

Sometimes a marriage of convenience
can be very inconvenient...
especially when love develops!

Terms of Engagement

Two full-length novels from two favorite Harlequin®
authors—at one astonishingly low price!

KATE HOFFMANN
MIRANDA LEE

Look for it in March 2002—wherever books are sold.

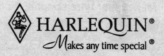

HARLEQUIN®
Makes any time special®

Visit us at www.eHarlequin.com

BR2TOE

The Shannon Sisters

A Trilogy by C.J. Carmichael

The stories of three sisters from Alberta whose lives and loves are as rocky—and grand—as the mountains they grew up in.

A *Second-Chance* Proposal

A murder, a bride-to-be left at the altar, a reunion. Is Cathleen Shannon willing to take a second chance on the man involved in these?

A *Convenient* Proposal

Kelly Shannon feels guilty about what she's done, and Mick Mizzoni feels that he's his brother's keeper—a volatile situation, but maybe one with a convenient way out!

A *Lasting* Proposal

Maureen Shannon doesn't want risks in her life anymore. Not after everything she's lived through. But Jake Hartman might be proposing a sure thing....

On sale starting February 2002

Available wherever Harlequin books are sold.

HARLEQUIN®

Makes any time special ®

HSRSS